By E. X. Ferrars

SLEEP OF THE UNJUST

E · X · FERRARS

Sleep ———————————

of the Unjust ————

———————————————

DOUBLEDAY
New York   London   Toronto   Sydney   Auckland

PUBLISHED BY DOUBLEDAY
a division of Bantam Doubleday Dell Publishing Group, Inc.
666 Fifth Avenue, New York, New York 10103

DOUBLEDAY and the portrayal of an anchor
with a dolphin are trademarks of Doubleday,
a division of Bantam Doubleday Dell
Publishing Group, Inc.

Library of Congress Cataloging-in-Publication Data

Ferrars, E. X.
Sleep of the unjust / E. X. Ferrars.—1st ed. in the U.S.A.
    p.   cm.
I. Title.
PR6003.R458S55   1991
823'.912—dc20   90-27454
CIP

ISBN 0-385-41707-1
Copyright © 1990 by M. D. Brown
All Rights Reserved
Printed in the United States of America
August 1991
First Edition in the United States of America

·   10 9 8 7 6 5 4 3 2 1

SLEEP OF THE UNJUST

One

THE FIRST THING that I had to do on Thursday morning was to go out and buy a wedding present for Sonia Capel.

This was more difficult than it may sound because I hardly knew her. It was her aunt, Christine Appleyard, who was my friend and who had insisted that I must come to the wedding. I am not very fond of weddings, perhaps because my own marriage had turned out not too well. True, the ceremony then had been a brief affair in a registry office with no one present but Felix, my husband of the time, myself, and two friends who had come as witnesses. We had all provided the appropriate signatures, then the four of us had had a very good lunch together in L'Etoile in Charlotte Street, then Felix and I had gone back to the home in Little Carbery Street in Bloomsbury, which we had already been occupying for some months and there had taken up life as before.

Naturally there had been hardly any wedding presents and I had already begun to wonder what madness it had been that had made me agree to tying a legal noose round my neck even after I had begun to find out what kind of man Felix was. I think it was an act of faith, that if we committed ourselves in what seemed such a final way we might still be able to make something of the relationship. And since it lasted for three years after our marriage, perhaps it did make some difference. But by then I had really had enough and managed to make up my mind to return to Allingford to the house in Ellsworthy Street, which my mother had left me when she died, and I was lucky enough to get back my old part-time job as a physiotherapist at the clinic where I had worked before I met Felix. And it had been when Christine Appleyard had appeared as a patient of mine at the clinic that I had first met her and we had by degrees drifted into friendship.

I had met her niece Sonia a few times, but she was a reserved young woman, very intelligent, I was sure, but whose interests and tastes I really knew nothing about, and buying a present for her, because Christine had insisted that I must come to her wedding, was the sort of problem that has a way of upsetting me. The dread of giving something that will be hopelessly unwelcome no doubt becomes more important to me than it need be. Like everyone else I have sometimes had to find tactful ways of disposing of sadly unwanted gifts, but when one is giving something oneself, vanity makes one want to be the one person who manages to provide just the very thing for which its recipient has been longing. To make things more complicated on this occasion, I could not afford to spend very much and the Appleyards happened to be very rich people.

I do not mean that they were in the class that owns yachts, private helicopters, and luxurious villas in exotic tax-havens. In fact, they did not own a single Rolls Royce. But they lived in a very beautiful Queen Anne mansion a little way out of Allingford, had two or three servants, a swimming-pool, and several acres of well-tended parkland. Christine's husband, George, was on the board of Arne

Webster Pharmaceuticals and on several other boards as well that I knew less about. It happened that I knew a certain amount about Arne Webster because one of their laboratories, of which I believed there were at least half a dozen dotted about the country, was on the outskirts of Allingford and I had occasionally met a number of the people who worked there.

George spent a certain amount of his time there too, though most of his work was in London. Sonia, I knew, was an orphan, so it was natural that she should be married from the Appleyards' home. I had been invited for the week-end and was to drive out there on Friday, the wedding being on the Saturday morning. So by Thursday it had really become urgent for me to go out and buy that present for Sonia, and at last, after a glance at my latest bank-statement and with my cheque-book in my handbag, I set out.

It was a fine June morning. There were roses in bloom in my little garden and a sprawling pink clematis and some rhododendrons. As I drove off my spirits began to rise. After all, if one gets into the right mood for it, there is something very enjoyable about buying a present. The danger is, of course, that one will choose something that one would like to be given oneself, yet perhaps that is as good a guide as any.

In the end I bought a small circular silver tray, the kind of thing on which one can take round drinks to one's guests if one has only three or four of them. The antique dealer from whom I bought it said that it was Georgian, and for all I knew he might have been speaking the truth, though as its price was rather modest I had my doubts. In any case, it was a pretty thing, and if Sonia had no use for it she could easily push it to the back of a cupboard and forget its existence. I went home, had some sherry and a

sandwich for lunch, then went to the clinic for the afternoon as I had several appointments there. Next morning,
at about half-past ten, I set off for Oldenham House, the
Appleyards' mansion.

I had been told that it had once been a rectory, but if
that was true any rector who had inhabited it must have
had far more in the way of an income than he could ever
have received from his parish. Not that it was really so very
big, but it stood on a slight rise above the little hamlet of
Oldenham, which added to its dignity. It was a longish
building, two storeys high, with another storey, almost
hidden behind a stone parapet, of low-ceilinged attics
where once a large staff of servants would have slept. The
present servants still slept there, Mrs. Grantly, the cook-
housekeeper, and a maid called Martha, who seemed to do
a little of everything and who dominated the household
because it would have been so uncomfortable for everyone
if she were to leave. Bob, a young man who was chauffeur
and handyman and who sometimes tidied himself up and
performed as butler, had a room over the garage.

I was inclined to think that these attics were the pleas-
antest rooms in the house. It was true that their ceilings
were sloping and their windows small, but from those
small windows it was possible to see across meadows and
woodland to the shining streak of the Olden, a placid little
river, flowing between overhanging willows. It was possible, looking out, to imagine that the countryside had not
changed for generations, because the motorway which by-
passed Allingford and ran only a little way beyond the
stream was in a deep cleft and was invisible from the
house, while it was just far enough away for the incessant
roar of traffic that came from it to be inaudible.

The house was built of softly mellowed red brick and
had two rows of tall, white-framed windows and a curved

portico that jutted out above a high, noble door. Such utilitarian things as garages, sheds of various kinds, and a small bungalow where guests were sometimes accommodated were all at the back of the house and were not to be seen by anyone approaching by the drive from the narrow road that led to Oldenham. It was about eleven o'clock when I arrived there, as Christine had told me to come early, and had my old Vauxhall taken over by Bob and driven away round the house after he had deposited my suitcase in the portico and vigorously rung the doorbell for me.

The door was opened at once by a girl whom I had never seen before. She looked about twenty, was about five foot tall, had a small, oval face, big, bright brown eyes, and a bush of tawny curls. She was wearing an unusually long full-skirted dress of flowered cotton, sandals, and large green plastic ear-rings.

She gave me an enchanting smile and said, "Good morning, you are Mrs. Freer, please?"

She had a strong foreign accent.

"Yes," I said.

"I am Ilse, the *au pair,*" she said. "I take your luggage, thank you." She snatched up my suitcase. "You come this way, please."

She set off at a trot towards the staircase. But before I had taken more than two or three steps after her a door opened and Christine came out. She gave me a hug and kissed me.

"It's so good to see you, Virginia!" she exclaimed. "My head's going round and round with all the absurd things that are happening. You'll help to keep me sane."

"What's so absurd?" I asked.

"This wedding! A church wedding. A white wedding. A wedding dress. A wedding cake. All the trimmings, and

Sonia and David are actually going away on a honeymoon together. And everyone knows they've been living together perfectly happily for at least two years. Can you think of anything more ridiculous?"

"It's the sort of thing that's liable to bite the young from time to time," I said. "They're afraid they may have missed something."

"It's a farce, my dear, an utter farce," Christine said, "and the worst thing about it is that I'm having to do all the hard work. Think of everything, order everything, invite people and make sure they're actually going to come, persuade our dear little vicar to officiate even though we hardly ever go to his church, and lay in lots of food that probably won't get eaten. And pretend! My God, how I've been pretending for the last few weeks! I mean, that I think it's simply splendid that Sonia and David are going to get married at last, when really I couldn't care less. By the way, this is Ilse Weigel from Zurich. She's a great friend of Fran's."

Ilse Weigel put down my suitcase and advanced on me with outstretched hand. I felt how muscular her grasp was.

"Hi!" she said gravely, sounding a little like a Red Indian warrior greeting an officer of the American army. "How do you do?"

I answered, "How do you do?"

She snatched up my suitcase again and shot up the curved, elegant staircase.

"I expect you'd like to get settled into your room," Christine said, and she and I followed the leaping girl. "I'm so glad you were able to come early as I suggested. With such weather I thought you might like a swim before lunch. It's turned out such a lovely morning, but one never knows what it may be like by the afternoon. Have you brought your swimming things?"

I had, though it had been a last-minute thought to jam them into my suitcase. I am not much given to swimming in our climate, but it was true that the morning was unusually sunny and warm and I had suddenly remembered that the Appleyards had a swimming-pool, so it had seemed worth while to take the things even if it should turn out that they would not be needed.

Christine took me into a room on the first floor which overlooked the pool. The room had two tall windows with pale green curtains, a darker green carpet, and white-painted furniture. There were flowers on a table between the windows. It was simple and cheerful. Ilse had deposited my suitcase on a rack under one of the windows and had shot out of the room. When I started unpacking I saw the pool, looking a very clear shining blue in the sunlight, with several people bobbing about in the water.

"They're all down there," Christine said. "Fran and Sonia and David and Paul—he's a friend of Fran's—and I wouldn't be surprised if my father's there too. You know them all, don't you? No, of course you've never met Fran, or Paul either, I suppose. Fran got home about a month ago. It's wonderful to have her back again."

Fran was Christine's daughter, and it was true that I had never met her. When I had first met Christine, Fran had still been at boarding-school, then she had spent a year in Zurich, the time, presumably, when she and Ilse had become friends. I knew nothing about Paul, whoever he was. But I knew Christine's father, old General Searle, who lived with the Appleyards.

"I suppose there are a lot more guests coming to the wedding," I said.

"Dozens—oh, my God, there are dozens!" Christine

cried. "Not staying here, however, and even David and Paul aren't actually sleeping here. You see, everything's got to be done properly, and it wouldn't be proper for the bridegroom to spend the night in the same house as the bride, so he and Paul are staying in The Barley Mow, the pub in the village. Isn't it all perfectly ridiculous?"

"I believe you're enjoying every minute of it," I said.

She laughed. She had a thin, pale, normally rather expressionless face that lit up wonderfully when she laughed. She was a very thin woman, the greyhound type, a few inches taller than me, and a little older. Her hair was very fair and was drawn sleekly back from her face into a roll at the back of her small head. Her eyes were large, dark grey, and fringed with long, dark lashes. She was wearing jeans and a white open-necked shirt which I noticed must be a man's because its buttons fastened the wrong way for a woman's. Perhaps it was one of George's. It was like her to have snatched up one of his if it happened to be handy when the weather suddenly became warm. She was always dressed carelessly, yet somehow managed to bestow a kind of distinction on the muddle of things that she wore.

"Perhaps I am enjoying it in a way," she said, "though you don't know how glad I'll be when it's all over. There's just one thing I wish. . . ." She paused and her face became melancholy. "Wouldn't it have been nice if Andrew could have been here? I wrote to him as soon as the whole thing became definite, sort of hoping that he'd make a point of coming. After all, he and Sonia and David used to be such good friends. But he didn't even answer my letter."

Andrew Appleyard was one of the problems of the family. He was a moderately successful film actor who for some years had been living in Hollywood. He had never quite achieved the status of a star, yet his dark, narrow, handsome face was familiar to most film-goers though under the name of Jon Sanchez, a nationally ambiguous name which went with the not very convincing foreign accent in which he usually spoke. The family regarded him as rather more of a success than he really was, feeling in a slightly surprised way that Appleyards on the whole did not make notable names for themselves. But they were shyly proud of him, though trying not to reveal how much hurt they were by the way that he had broken all his ties with them once he had achieved what he had.

He was about ten years older than Fran and about the same age as Sonia. He, Sonia, and David Eldred had all been at Oxford together, then Andrew had plunged into films, Sonia had acquired a research job with the BBC, and David had made a good name for himself as a biochemist with the firm of Arne Webster Pharmaceuticals. He and Sonia had a flat in London, but he worked for some of his time in the branch of the firm in Allingford and had always spent a good deal of time with the Appleyards in Oldenham. I had met him two or three times, but I knew him even less than I knew Sonia.

Unpacking my suitcase, I came on the little silver tray that I had bought for them and gave it to Christine, who exclaimed that it was charming and took it away with her while I hung up the good dress that I had brought for the wedding and changed into my swimming-suit and the towelling wrap that I had brought. I knew my way to the pool and presently followed Christine down to it. It was reached by french windows that opened out of the drawing-room. These stood open now, and on the terrace outside them several lounging chairs stood about, in one of which I saw the long, bony, tough-looking figure of General Searle, a tall, white-haired man of about eighty who was wearing dark blue swimming trunks which covered a good deal more of him than did those of the young man who was talking to him. I had never seen the young man before, so deduced that he was probably Paul, Fran's friend whom I had not yet met.

The General saw me and levered himself cautiously on to his feet to greet me. His movements were slow and stiff, but his shorts were wet, so it looked as if, in spite of some arthritis, he still went in for a certain amount of swimming. He shook me by the hand and told me how delighted he was to see me, as he was sure that I would give Christine the support that she needed.

"And this is Paul Camrose," he said, drawing the young man forward. "He's going to be best man at the ceremony and I'm giving the bride away. Paul, this is our very good friend, Mrs. Freer, whom I'm sure Christine has told you about."

Paul Camrose gave me a pleasant smile and said, "Oh yes, indeed."

He was tall and broad-shouldered with a look of relaxed and cheerful self-confidence. His hair was thick, dark, and curly, his forehead high and broad, his nose short, and his mouth wide, showing very fine even white teeth when he smiled. His eyes were dark and large and bright. In fact, he was a very good-looking young man, aged perhaps about twenty-seven or eight.

"Going in swimming?" he asked. "I shouldn't put it off for too long. The forecast isn't very good and one never knows with this climate of ours when the sun's going to go in."

It happened that at the moment there was not a cloud in the sky and the sunshine on the terrace was deliciously warm, and when I kicked off my sandals the tiles around the pool felt almost scorching. But his advice seemed good and I made my way to the diving-board at one end of it. I am not much of a diver but I prefer going into the water more or less head first to crawling inch by inch down some slippery steps. There were two or three other people in the pool, and one of them I recognized as Sonia Capel, who had just surfaced after a dive with her golden hair dripping. I stepped out on to the end of the diving-board and plunged.

Almost at once, before I had reached the surface, I encountered something solid. It was a body, male. Whoever it was wriggled away from me in a hurry, and both he and I, facing each other, prepared to apologize for having bumped so hard into the other.

But what I said was, "No! No, what in hell are you doing here?"

"Didn't they tell you I'd be here?" Felix, my one-time husband, said. "How very careless of them."

Two

I VERY SELDOM CALL FELIX my ex-husband because we never troubled to get around to a divorce, so he is my husband still. If either of us had ever wanted to venture on marriage again, I suppose that we should have had to do something about it, but though we had each been near it once or twice the final step had not been taken. And as long as it does not happen too often and our meetings do not last for too long, I enjoy a certain amount of his company.

Though in his middle forties he is still good-looking, in his own way is entertaining, and is really a generous and kindly man. If only he could have stuck occasionally to telling the truth about himself instead of trying to impress people with utterly fantastic fables, and if it had not been for one or two other disconcerting habits that he had, I expect I should have stuck to him and loved him very much. I still had a kind of affection for him, and after recovering from the first shock of encountering him in the swimming-pool, I began to feel quite glad that, like me, he appeared to be a wedding-guest.

"But what are you doing here?" I asked again.

"Don't you remember, Sonia's an old friend of mine?"

he said. "We've known each other for years. I came down yesterday evening."

I remembered then that it had really been because of Sonia that Christine had come to me as a patient when she started having unpleasant pains in her back. When Sonia had heard from Felix that I worked in Allingford, and after he had given me a glowing recommendation, as he was always liable to do, Christine had persuaded her doctor that she ought to give me a trial. I believe I did her a certain amount of good, though I had a suspicion that the trouble might have cleared up anyhow. She had been in a state of stress which I believed was connected with her son Andrew, and as she came gradually to accept his rejection of his family the pain had lessened. She occasionally came back to the clinic even now, but not as often as we saw each other in Ellsworthy Street or in Oldenham House as friends.

"Are you staying for the week-end?" I asked Felix.

"Yes, I'm in that guest-bungalow at the back of the house," he answered. "The house itself is overflowing."

He pushed his wet hair back from his face. It was thick and fair and he had thick, fair eyebrows above vivid blue eyes with curiously drooping eyelids which made them look almost triangular. His face was almost triangular too, wide at the temples, pointed at the chin. He was slender and only of medium height. As both of us were treading water in the pool we appeared to be about equally tall, though in fact he is an inch or two more so than I am.

"And will you tell me just what you're supposed to be doing at the moment?" I said. "Just so that I don't say anything tactless."

When we had married I had believed him to be a civil engineer, working for a big construction firm, only to discover a little later that they had never heard of him and that he was really working for a very shady firm of second-hand car dealers whose managing director happened to be in gaol for fraud. But Felix had claimed to be all sorts of other things since then, sometimes conferring titles on himself, such as a knighthood or a professorship or some notable military rank, and while he was at it changing his name from time to time. An air of boyish charm, which had lasted him well into his thirties, had gradually given way to an air of distinction which made it easy for him to make strangers believe that he was just what he claimed to be. Sonia, of course, was no stranger to him, and probably knew better than I did what he was doing at the moment.

"Suppose we get out of this," he said instead of answering. "I think I see drinks arriving."

Ilse, pushing a trolley with bottles and glasses on it, had just appeared on the terrace. I began to move towards the end of the pool, where the steps were. Felix stayed beside me.

"Well, what are you doing?" I asked again.

"At the moment, strictly speaking, I'm unemployed," he said. "I did very well out of the last job I had. I was a guide at a stately home belonging to an Arab, and the pay was excellent. So I'm treating myself to a rest, except that now and then I do a little freelance journalism. I've discovered I've a knack for writing travel articles for a paper called *The Grail*. You've probably never heard of it, but it brings in the odd bob or two."

"But isn't that a religious paper?" I asked, the name in fact evoking a faint memory.

"What's wrong with that?" he asked.

"You aren't particularly religious."

"Nor are most of the other contributors. Anyway, they've never worried me about that, they just happen to like what I write."

"And you've never done any travelling."

That was perhaps the more serious criticism. Felix rarely went more than a hundred miles or so from London. He was frightened of aeroplanes, claiming that this was because of claustrophobia, due to his often having been locked in a dark cupboard in his childhood as a punishment by his father, and at sea he was always horribly sick. So living as he did on an island, it really seemed best for him to stay at home, though naturally that might change if ever the Channel tunnel is finished. But nothing will stop him telling those who do not know him how he once crossed the Greenland ice-cap alone on skis and how he had been lost in the desert in Australia and been rescued by a tribe of aborigines who had stolen his clothes so that he had to go naked for weeks, and fed him on maggots but had saved his life. A few such stories, I supposed, had interested the editor of *The Grail,* for he really told them very convincingly.

"I read plenty of travel books," he said, "and I watch all the travel and wildlife programmes on television. It really isn't so very difficult."

"So you two have met," Sonia said, suddenly appearing just ahead of us at the steps. "I knew you'd enjoy that."

There was a sardonic smile on her face. She was a tall, slim girl with long fair hair that now coiled wetly on her shoulders, an oval face with strong, firmly formed features, grey eyes, and something about her that I had always found faintly formidable. She was self-contained and usually almost aloof, and not inclined to assert herself. She was about twenty-seven. She was wearing the briefest of bikinis.

"Of course we shall," Felix said. "It was a splendid idea of Christine's to ask us both."

"Of course, she always hopes that some day you'll make things up again."

Sonia was climbing up the steps. I followed her and Felix followed me.

"Be that as it may," he said, "we're both immensely looking forward to tomorrow. Was the wedding her idea too?"

"No, I thought that for once in my life I'd like to be the star of a really good production," she said. "I shall be the star, of course. David will only be in a supporting role."

"How lucky then that your cousin Andrew couldn't come," Felix said, "because of course he'd have stolen the show."

"That's true, we might even have had camera men here," she said, wringing water out of her dripping hair as she stood beside the pool. "But I'm sorry about it really, because Christine would so have loved to have him. It's five or six years since she saw him last and he almost never writes to her. A card at Christmas saying he hopes she and George are well, and that's about that."

"And he was always her favourite, wasn't he, rather than Fran?" I said.

Fran had been in the pool but had climbed out of it ahead of us and was standing beside her grandfather with a glass of the sherry that Ilse had brought out. She was eighteen, I remembered Christine had told me, almost ten years younger than her brother, a small, slender girl with dark hair cropped short except for a swirl of it across her forehead and delicately arched eyebrows above bright dark eyes.

She introduced herself to me. "I'm Fran," she said. "I know you're Virginia. Will you have some sherry, or d'you prefer gin and tonic or Campari soda?"

I chose my usual sherry and she poured out a glass for me.

"Are you going to be staying at home now?" I asked.

"Oh yes," she said, then she seemed to hesitate. "Yes," she repeated, "though I haven't really thought of what I'm going to do. I don't suppose I'll just stay at home and do nothing. But I'm not a bit clever. If I try to get a job it'll probably turn out to be something horribly boring. I believe I could manage to be somebody's secretary, but unless it was someone exciting, like, say, a criminal lawyer, I don't suppose I'd stick to it."

"You're drawn to crime, are you?" I asked, wondering if she was thinking of Perry Mason and Della Street.

"Well, I don't exactly mean that," she said. "I just gave that as an example. I expect a lot of the work even with someone like that would be horribly dreary, wills and buying and selling property and investing people's money for them and things like that."

Christine joined us. She was still in her jeans and shirt and had plainly not been in the pool.

"There's no need for her to think of doing anything special at the moment," she said. "We can put up with having her living at home for a little, though of course she may find that horribly boring like everything else. George doesn't think she should look for a job yet."

George Appleyard was not in the group beside the pool. I guessed that he was probably still in London at one of his committees and would not be home till the evening.

"And he's quite right," General Searle said. "She doesn't need the money. If she takes a job she'll just be doing some poor girl out of it who really does need it. Anyway, she'll probably get married before she's even half-trained."

"That doesn't mean I shan't want a job," Fran said with

defiance in her voice. "Most of the married girls I know
have jobs."

"Just wait till the babies start arriving," he said. "That's
a job in itself."

She flushed a little as she turned away, as if this flippant
remark had some embarrassing meaning for her.

David Eldred drifted up to me just then and said,
"Hello." That's a very nice tray you've brought us, Virginia. Thank you very much. Have you seen our display of
presents?"

He was a tall, almost gauntly thin young man of about
thirty, with untidy fair hair which looked as if it was as
long as it was because he had forgotten to have it cut, even
though he was to be married tomorrow, rather than because he was aiming at any particular fashion. He wore
large circular spectacles which were faintly tinted so that it
was difficult to be sure if his eyes were grey or blue. He
had a long face with sharp features and an air, when he
spoke to one, of finding it difficult not to let his thoughts
drift away. I knew that for a short time after taking his
degree he had had a job in a Midland university, but then
he had moved to where the money was in industry. He
had landed his job with Arne Webster at least partly
through his friendship with Sonia.

"No, not yet," I said. "Christine must show it to me."

"We've done very well, considering," he said. He meant
considering the fact that it was well known that he and
Sonia had been sharing that flat in London for the last
couple of years and which presumably was adequately furnished and not in need of presents to make it habitable. I
agreed with Christine that the wedding tomorrow was little more than a masquerade. I wondered if Sonia would
have the gall to have a real wedding-dress, perhaps even a
veil. He went on, "George has been complaining that the

smell of an upper-middle-class wedding is mothballs. If you're really upper class the suit you wear for the occasion doesn't smell of mothballs because you wear it often enough at Ascot and wherever not to have to put it away in safety, and if you're a bit lower down the scale, you don't smell of anything because of course you've got your suit from Moss Bros, as in fact I have. But the family here is just on that social and economic level whose morning coats have a strong smell of insecticide."

"I'd like to see the presents," I said, sipping my sherry. "Where are they?"

"In the library, so-called," David answered. "Very nicely arranged by Christine. Poor Christine, the whole thing is horribly hard on her. Of course, it would have been in far better taste if Sonia and I had gone away quietly to a registry office somewhere, perhaps with you and Felix as witnesses, once we'd decided we honestly wanted to tie the knot. But there's a streak of the dramatic that goes right through this family. Andrew isn't simply a freak who got his talent from nowhere. It's in his blood. Did you know that Christine and her sister, Sonia's mother, started life as actresses? It was only marriage that put a stop to it for both of them. And Sonia, with her BBC research job, is really the moth getting as close to the flame as she dares."

Beside me Felix misquoted, "The fault, dear Brutus, is not in our stars, but in our genes. I'd like to see the presents too, David."

"Let's go and look at them," I said.

I finished my sherry, towelled myself dry, put on my wrap and sandals, and headed for the library.

When David had called it a so-called library, what he had meant was that there were very few books in it and most of them were paperbacks. George was an obsessive reader of detective stories and most of one wall of the room was covered with shelf on shelf filled with them. The opposite wall was covered with complete sets of classics, very well bound but with a sadly unread look about them. Christine, I knew, relied for most of her reading on the public library in Allingford and was one of the people who are liable to say with a touch of pride that they hardly ever read novels but prefer biography and travel. Who had collected all those neglected classics I did not know, unless it had been George's father. It was he who had bought the house and furnished it, and except for occasional lapses into modernity, due to Christine's erratic taste, it was still very much as he had left it.

The presents were laid out on a couple of long tables, and I saw my little silver tray among them. Most of the presents were ornamental rather than useful, though a few friends who appeared not to have known that Sonia had been housekeeping for some time, and presumably had all she needed for this, had supplied things like stainless steel cooking-pots, casseroles, and some deadly looking kitchen cutlery. But mostly what I saw were vases of fine glass, some carved ivory figures, a few pictures of varying attractiveness, and other such things. There were cards attached to them, and I saw that General Searle had contributed a handsome canteen of silver and Christine a Copenhagen dinner service. Before I had discovered what George had presented, Felix was saying to me, "Look, this is what I brought. What do you think of it?"

He had picked up a small object that looked like jade and was holding it out for me to see. It seemed to be a kind of lizard, or perhaps a dragon, and if it really was jade was probably valuable.

"Where did you nick it?" I asked.

It is one of Felix's more unfortunate characteristics that

he is a skilled and dedicated shop-lifter. It was one of the things about him that I had not yet discovered when we married. I had merely thought that with all his faults he was an extraordinarily generous man, keeping me supplied with an almost inexhaustible stream of presents. And he really was very generous and loved giving presents and almost always gave away the things that he slipped deftly into a pocket when he was out shopping. Once I had discovered that he did this, I had tried to convince him that it was a crime and that if I accepted any of his gifts I should be liable to prosecution as a receiver of stolen property, but I had never made any impression on him. He thought of what he did more as a kind of sport, himself against the establishment, than as serious law-breaking, and I have to admit my worst fears about it were really not moral but came mostly from a dread that he would be caught. However that had never happened yet.

"Let me tell you, I paid for it in good solid cash," he said, and what he answered might even be true, for he did occasionally speak the truth, which was confusing. "It's Chinese, I think."

He put the little dragon back on the table.

"Here's a very pretty thing," he said.

He was right, it was very pretty. It was a necklace made of a slender gold chain with a pendant attached to it consisting of a single large pearl held in a claw of small diamonds. A card said that it was a present from George.

"Coming from George, one can assume it's genuine," Felix said.

"Of course," I agreed.

"I don't suppose they've actually gone to the length of having a security guard to look after the things till tomorrow," he said thoughtfully.

"Felix!" I exclaimed. "It hasn't by any chance crossed your mind. . . ."

But I stopped there because, to do him justice, I had never known him to steal from friends. Even if he coveted the necklace, perhaps to give to whatever woman he was interested in at the moment, I did not think that there was any risk that he would help himself to it.

He strolled on along the table, stopping here and there to look at something that had caught his attention. Then Ilse came suddenly into the room.

"Lunch, please," she said. "In ten minutes. You get dressed perhaps or you stay like you are, Mrs. Appleyard say you do what you like best."

I decided to get dressed and went up to my bedroom.

After lunch Sonia, who had put on jeans and a shirt, slipped her arm through mine and said, "Come upstairs and see my dress." In a lower voice, as we were going up, she added, "Don't look so worried, it hasn't got a train."

In fact, when she showed it to me, it did not look like a wedding-dress at all. It was white except for a design of small red speckles and a red belt and it was very simple and looked expensive, but it was just a pretty dress that could be worn on all sorts of occasions. She produced from her wardrobe a small red hat that matched the belt, combed back her long fair hair, and perched the hat on top of it.

"There!" she said, turning to me with one of her sardonic smiles. "What do you think of it?"

I thought it very attractive and said so, though I added that it did not go too well with jeans.

"D'you know, this is the first hat I've owned for I don't know how many years," she said. "When I was at school I had to wear a hat with the school badge on it, but really we only wore those for the journey down there and the journey home. I expect you wore hats quite a lot when you were younger."

"Never very often, as a matter of fact," I said, "though I remember a time when, if I was feeling specially depressed, I'd suddenly go and buy myself a new one. And they were hardly ever a success and I'd go back to my old head-scarf."

"I hope you didn't feel you'd have to wear one tomorrow" she said.

"I did wonder about it, but I don't possess such a thing at the moment," I said, "and I didn't feel like spending a lot of money on one that I'd probably never wear again. Nice ones are a fearful price nowadays. But with Christine talking about a white wedding and so on, I began to feel I ought to have done something about it."

She laughed. "You know Christine. I know I told you I wanted it, but if it hadn't been for her David and I would have done the reasonable thing and gone to a registry office and never talked about it to anyone. We're thinking of having children, you see, and if you do that I think it's best to get married."

"But she gave me the impression a white wedding was all your idea," I said. "She even called it ridiculous."

"Oh, of course she would." Sonia took off the hat, put it back in the wardrobe, and dropped down on the edge of the bed. There was one easy chair in the room, and as I foresaw that she wanted to talk, I sat down in it. "She won't admit it, but she wanted it so badly," she went on. "I don't mean merely that David and I should get married, that's understandable, but as a kind of compensation for something that happened when I was quite young—well, about twenty-two. I nearly got married then and she'd begun to plan all the celebrations, and then—well it didn't happen. It was my fault really, letting her go as far as she did, when I didn't know my own mind. We'd even chosen the material for my dress when I suddenly did a bolt. I went to Italy and insisted on staying there till my money ran out. Then I came home, but of course there was no more talk of a marriage and I got my job with the BBC and then later there was David. And if she's calling this whole thing tomorrow ridiculous, I suppose it's a kind of insurance in case I should do anything of the same sort again."

"And is there the slightest chance that you might?"

She shook her head, smiling. But in spite of the smile there was a curious sadness in her face.

"Oh no, I'm quite a grown-up girl by now," she said. "I don't do things like that."

But she was only about twenty-seven or eight, I thought, and if she had been twenty-two when she had fled from marriage, that was only five of so years ago. A long time for the young, perhaps, but it was longer than that since Felix and I had separated and the distress of that still seemed strangely recent. I should have liked to ask Sonia who it was whom she had so nearly married, but as she did not seem inclined to offer the information I thought it might be best not to do so.

"So you want children," I said.

"Oh yes, we both do," she answered. "About three or four. And if it turns out that for some reason we can't have any, I think we'll adopt, though a psychiatrist friend of ours warned us that it can be a fearful mistake. He says you're liable to get the child of a mentally retarded mother and an irresponsible father. All the same, I think it's what we shall do."

"You aren't by any chance pregnant now?" I asked. "That isn't the real reason why all this is happening?"

"No, but I did have a miscarriage some time ago," she

said, "and David got it into his head that perhaps it happened because I didn't feel secure, living as we were, and perhaps he was right. As a matter of fact . . ." She paused and I thought that she did not mean to go on, but then she added in a tone of real or assumed indifference, I was not sure which, "I've had two miscarriages."

"So that's why you've been thinking about adopting."

"Yes. Do you think it would be a mistake?"

"Oh, for God's sake, don't ask me anything like that!" I exclaimed. It had been something for which I had been profoundly thankful that Felix and I had never had children, but the urge to have them had never been very strong in me. "It isn't the sort of thing about which I'd dare to give anyone any advice."

"No, I suppose you wouldn't. Well, do you like my dress?"

That seemed a much safer subject.

"It's charming. Now I think, if you don't mind, I'm going to lie down for a little. That swim seems to have made me awfully sleepy."

I very seldom sleep in the afternoon and perhaps it really was the swim that affected me, for I fell sound asleep as soon as I lay down on my bed. I slept until after five o'clock, and when I woke it took me a moment to remember where I was. Then I noticed that the sky had clouded over and that a light rain was falling against the windows. I felt a certain inclination to remain where I was rather than to go downstairs and encounter the family and their guests, including Felix, again. I am used to spending a good deal of time by myself and I often find the pressure of people round me very tiring. But simply disappearing for too long I supposed would be discourteous, so I got up, changed my dress, combed my hair, put on a little fresh make-up, and went downstairs.

I found that everyone else had already assembled in the drawing-room and had begun on drinks. George was there and gave me a kiss and brought me a glass of sherry. He was a tall, somewhat portly man of nearly sixty. He had heavy features, long, heavy cheeks, and the beginnings of a double chin. His eyes were dark, spaced far apart and were slightly protuberant, which gave them a rather startled, staring look. In fact, I did not think that he was a man whom it was easy to startle. His hair was grey and was thin on top of his head, though he was not yet actually bald. He was in a dark blue suit which looked oddly formal among all the other people there. I supposed that he had only just returned from London. He had always been friendly to me, though in a remote sort of way, as if he was not really sure what I was doing there. I generally half-expected, when we met, that it would turn out that he had forgotten my name.

However, he had never actually done so, and he greeted me now, "Ah, Virginia. Good to see you."

I said that it was good to see him and added, "That's a very pretty necklace you've given Sonia. I'm sure it's the nicest of all her presents."

"You think so?" he said, his full-lipped mouth stretching in a smile. "Good, good. It belonged to my mother and I've another of hers I'm keeping for Fran. She can have it for her twenty-first birthday or her wedding, whichever happens first, though for all I know, she'll think it's hopelessly out of fashion. But I suppose, even if it is, it'll come in again in the next twenty years or so. Pretty girl, isn't she?"

He looked with affectionate pride at Fran, who was talking to Paul Camrose. They were standing near the french window which was still open in spite of the rain. I could see the raindrops splashing in the swimming-pool. But the evening was still very warm.

"You know, of course, I've never met her before," I said, "or Paul either. What does he do?"

"He's in the accountancy department of Arne Webster, here in Allingford," George answered. "A very promising young fellow."

"Does he live in Allingford?"

"No, in London, and I think we may soon be moving him to London altogether. I think he could be useful there."

"But I gather Fran hasn't made up her mind what she wants to do."

"I believe not. She keeps having ideas about it and changing her mind. There's no hurry about it in any case—"

He was suddenly interrupted by Ilse erupting into the room in the explosive way she had.

"Please!" she cried loudly enough for everyone else there to become silent. "A man is there!"

"A man?" Christine said, looking bewildered. "What kind of man?"

"A man in a taxi."

But she had no need to add to this not very informative statement, for the man in question came into the room only a moment after her. I had no need to be told who he was. I had seen his dark, narrow, handsome face in I don't know how many films.

Christine gave a cry of "Andrew!" and rushed into his arms.

Three

I SUPPOSE it ought not to have surprised me, yet it did, when Andrew Appleyard, better known to the world as Jon Sanchez, said, "Mother, darling," that it was not in a semi-foreign accent but in as plain English as that of his parents. I was so used to seeing him as an Italianate gangster, or a Mexican bandit, or something else Latin and usually dubious, that it seemed strange to hear him speak in the accent fostered by his public school and Oxford. But this was as absurd of me as it would have been if I had been surprised at his not instantly producing a gun and come shooting his way into the room. Even though I was so used to him being the villain of the piece, I did not expect that of him, but the soft, pleasant, ordinary voice coming from him did seem strange.

He was not really as tall as he appeared in his films, perhaps not more than five foot ten, was slender, somewhat narrow shouldered, narrow hipped, and was dark haired and dark skinned enough to have come from the Mediterranean. His colouring, I realised, he had inherited from his father, for before George's hair had turned grey it had probably been black, to go by his eyebrows, which were still finely formed black arches over his dark, protuberant eyes. But Andrew's sharp, almost delicately modelled features had come from Christine.

Those protuberant eyes of George's, which usually had a way of looking faintly startled, looked really startled now.

"For God's sake, Andrew, why didn't you write?" he exclaimed. He had moved up beside Christine and as she released her son, he clapped him on the shoulder. "Come to think of it, you were always one for giving people surprises, weren't you? Bad habit really. Can so easily go wrong."

"Don't tell me this has gone wrong," Andrew said. "Honestly, I didn't know until yesterday that I could make it. An engagement got cancelled and I suddenly realised I'd just time to come over and be here for the great event. I did think of telephoning first, but I got confused about the difference in time and wasn't sure I wouldn't be waking you up in the middle of the night. So I just got on a plane and came. Sonia, my love, the best of everything to you and David."

It was only as he advanced into the room towards Sonia that I realised that in fact something had gone wrong with his surprise. No one but his parents had moved forward to greet him, and there was silence in the room. The sort of silence that is not produced by simple astonishment, but by tension. Only Felix, it seemed, was prepared to show any pleasure at seeing him. He came forward, holding out his hand.

"Remember me?" he said. "We knew each other quite well once."

"Felix, by God!" Andrew exclaimed, looking almost relieved at meeting someone who would welcome him. They shook hands warmly. "You're still around, are you, and haven't got pinched for anything? Those days in Little Carbery Street! Are you still there?"

"Yes, still at the old address," Felix said.

"And your wife—I mean, the girl who'd been your wife —we never met, I believe. How's she? Has either of you married again?"

"Here she is," Felix said, drawing me forward, and I found myself shaking hands with Andrew.

"So you've made it up, have you?" he asked.

"Well, yes and no," Felix said. "We haven't moved in together again, but we've agreed to have a high regard for one another."

"Ah, it's like that, is it?" Andrew said. Then he turned to Sonia. "I have the very highest regard for you, you know, my love." And putting both hands on her shoulders, he drew her to him and kissed her.

It was only the friendliest of kisses, a very light one on her cheek, but there was not a trace of an answering smile on her face and her body looked rigid, as if she were preparing to fight off a much more demanding embrace.

He kept his hands on her shoulders, but held her a little away from him.

"Can't you even say hallo to me?" he asked.

"Hallo," she murmured in an expressionless voice.

"And you, David?"

But before David could answer Fran darted forward and flung herself at her brother, throwing her arms round his neck.

"You don't even know me, do you, Andrew?" she cried. "I was only a little thing when you went away and you haven't recognized me because now I'm grown up. I'm Fran, Andrew. Don't you remember, you used to have a baby sister called Fran?"

She sounded profoundly amused at the absurdity of it.

"Fran!" he said, and let Sonia go and transferred his grasp to his sister. "Now why didn't anyone tell me we'd such a beauty in the family? I'd have been over long ago. Or you might have come out to me. Did you never think of that?"

"You're only saying that," she said. "You don't mean it."

I thought that she was right. There was suddenly something very artificial in his tone, as there had not been when he spoke to Sonia. But he said, "Ah no, I mean it. You must come out as soon as you can. Why don't you? Perhaps you could come back with me."

Paul moved a step forward.

"You won't make yourself very popular if you try to take her away from us when she's only just got home," he said. But he was smiling and his air of cheerful self-confidence, which for a moment had seemed disturbed, was back and he held out a hand to Andrew.

"Hallo, Paul," Andrew said casually as he took it. From his tone it might have been thought that they had met only a few days before, instead of several years. He did not seem very interested. It was still David to whom he wanted to speak. "Well, David, are you also going to say I'm not welcome?"

David seemed to find it difficult to bring his attention to bear on what was happening, though his tinted spectacles made it difficult to be sure what his expression really was. But the absent-minded air that I had noticed about him when I first met him had replaced the tension that momentarily had been his greeting to Andrew.

"Depends," he said. "Just why have you come, Andrew?"

"To see you married, of course," Andrew replied.

"No other reason?"

"Well, I've a certain desire to see my family."

"And that's all?"

"What else could there be?"

"I just thought you might have some other idea in mind."

"Now look, David—"

"All right, all right. That's all. That'll do."

"Time passes, doesn't it? Things change."

"If you say so."

It had taken me a moment to realise that they were quarrelling and that David, who appeared so easy-going, was in a state of quiet fury.

Christine appeared to have realised it, for she looked distressed. Slipping her arm through Andrew's, she said, "We'll have to find you somewhere to sleep. It'll have to be in the bungalow, as everywhere else is full up. Would you like to get settled in now or have a drink first?"

In a rather grim tone he answered, "Perhaps I'd better get settled in. It'll give you all time to get used to the fact that I'm here."

"Well, you really should have written, or telephoned, or something," she said. "You've taken us all so by surprise."

"That fact had struck me."

"Come along then. We must get Martha. She'll make up the bed. Felix is sleeping in the bungalow too."

She led Andrew out of the room to find the invaluable Martha, who ran the household.

When they had gone there was a short silence in the room, then Paul said, "He really didn't tell any of you he was coming?"

"No, but isn't it exciting?" Fran cried. "I think it's marvellous."

Sonia suddenly collapsed on a sofa and startled everyone by going into a fit of shrill, hysterical laughter. She pressed both her hands to her mouth, as if to choke it back, but her whole body shook.

David leant over her, gently patting her shoulder.

"It's all right," he said. "It doesn't matter."

She gave a gasp and sat upright.

"Time passes, he said," she said. "How right he is."

"All right then, there's nothing to worry about," he said, but there were lines of worry on his forehead.

"But he doesn't believe time passes." She grasped one of his hands and hung on to it with a look of desperation. "David, can we make him go away? He's going to spoil everything."

"Now, now," George said. "We don't want this sort of melodrama."

"But don't you understand, he's come on purpose to spoil things?" she said.

"Nonsense," he said. "He just came on impulse, and very nice of him too."

"It isn't nonsense. You'll see, it's why he's come."

I suppose that by then I had realised what the trouble was about. Sonia had told me that she had once nearly got married before, but had fled from that marriage to Italy. So it was fairly clear now, I thought, that the man whom she had almost married had been Andrew Appleyard, and that after her desertion of him, whatever had caused it, there had never been any reconciliation. His appearance on the scene now, she believed, was intended at the very least to cast gloom over an occasion that was to have been one of simple happiness. She thought that it was meant to stir feelings of guilt in her, perhaps even to doubt the wisdom of what she was doing.

I doubted if she could be right. As Andrew had said, time passes, and his time had been passed in an environment where there were almost certainly considerable numbers of young women who were far more beautiful than Sonia. It seemed to me probable that George was right that Andrew had come to her wedding on an impulse, just to effect the reconciliation that had not happened before.

But Felix was not altogether of my mind. The rain had stopped and he and I went for a stroll in the garden after dinner, which had been an uncomfortably sombre meal though Christine had done her best to chatter her way through it, and Fran and Paul had done what they could to help her, as the General also had. He had questioned Andrew closely about his work and tried to get him to say why he pretended to be a goddamned foreigner, talking that fake lingo, when he could talk perfectly good English.

Andrew had replied that it had been the physiognomy that he had inherited from his parents that had decided his fate, the dark colouring that had come from his father and the features from his mother, together, he had added, smiling, perhaps with something in himself that made him able to be convincingly sinister. I could not make up my mind if really there was not something a little sinister about him, though I am sure that this would never have occurred to me if I had not seen him cast so often as a villain and if the reaction to him of Sonia and David had been different. If they had simply shown pleasure at seeing him, that was all that I should have felt myself. But they seemed to have made up their minds that he had only come to their wedding to spoil it.

"That isn't impossible, you know." Felix said when I spoke of my feelings as we wandered through the garden, which had a sweet, fresh smell after the rain. "Whatever happened five or six years ago was pretty peculiar and I think it may always have left a bitter taste."

"Do you know what happened?" I asked.

"More or less, though I've never been quite able to explain it," he said. "I know Andrew and Sonia had an affair while they were still at Oxford. I met them through Paul, whom I'd known for some time, and they got into the habit of dropping in at Little Carbery Street when they wanted somewhere to stay overnight in London— you know the kind of thing—though we didn't really know each other fearfully well. But Paul told me Sonia and Andrew were going to get married and then suddenly it was all off and Sonia shot off to Italy on her own and stayed there for some months, and Andrew, who was just beginning to have a little success in films, took off for Hollywood. And I remember Paul saying something about Sonia having a miscarriage, so I thought it might all be something to do with post-natal depression or whatever they call it, or anyway that she'd gone a bit round the bend for the time being. But when she came home she seemed as normal as ever, if not more so, if you know what I mean. She seemed to have lost something purely young and cheerful and turned into the slightly stern sort of person she is now. Then the affair with David started and I assumed she'd got Andrew out of her system, whatever the trouble had really been. Only the way she's reacted to his turning up makes me wonder if she really has."

"You don't know if it was something he did that made her break that marriage off?" I asked.

Felix shook his head. "It isn't impossible. Infidelity, perhaps, though I never heard anything of that sort from Paul. My impression was that Andrew was crazy about her and jealous too. Perhaps that was what upset her. He may have been a bit too possessive for her liking, trying to stop her having quite normal friendships with other people.

But I really don't know. I only know that I wish he hadn't turned up at this particular moment."

"But he can't really do anything to upset the affair tomorrow, can he?"

"Except perhaps get on everyone's nerves."

We were both wrong, but we could not have foreseen that. Neither of us could have guessed what was to happen.

All that happened that evening was that Andrew went early to bed and both George and Christine seemed relieved by that, however glad they were to see him. There were two bedrooms in the guest-bungalow, and he and Felix had one each. Paul and David, who were to spend the night at The Barley Mow in the village, left for it about half-past ten. They had been given keys by the landlord, they said, so that they could come and go as they liked without worrying about closing time at the pub. I saw David and Sonia standing embraced on the terrace, saying good-night and arranging, I supposed, their meeting in the church tomorrow, but she looked strangely stiff in his arms, and when he wanted to kiss her on the lips she turned her head away and suddenly broke away from him. He stood there for a moment, looking helpless, then he turned to join Paul and the two of them set off down the drive towards the village.

The only person who seemed unequivocally glad to see Andrew was Fran. She joined me in the drawing-room, where I sat on for a little while after Felix had gone to the bungalow, and threw herself down on a sofa.

"I knew he'd come, you know," she said. "I felt it in my bones. Do you believe in telepathy?"

"I've never quite made up my mind," I said. "For every time that it seems to work there are several hundred times that it doesn't. Only each time that it does seem to work, it feels so very convincing, doesn't it?"

"Oh, I believe in it," she said. "I could give you dozens of instances when I've known exactly what someone else was thinking. And I've been thinking of Andrew off and on I don't know how often for the last week or two. I think I may have known even before he did that he'd come. Isn't he handsome?"

"Yes, I agree to that," I said.

"More, I think, in real life than when you see him on the screen. I suppose that's because they have to make him up to look a rather evil sort of character. I do hope he'll stay on here for a little while and not go back to America after a few days, as he was talking of doing."

"Will you go with him, if he does go?" I asked.

She laughed. "He didn't mean that. I'd only be in his way. Besides . . ." She paused.

"Yes?" I said.

She started to say something, seemed to change her mind, then went on casually, "If he really did mean it, perhaps I'd go, though I could hardly get organised, get a visa and all that sort of thing, in a few days, could I? But these bones of mine tell me he didn't mean it. Now good-night."

"Good-night," I said as she left me.

I went up to bed myself a few minutes later.

I had just reached the bottom of the stairs when Christine came out of the library and followed me up. She followed me into my room.

"Well, what do you think?" she asked, sitting down on the edge of the bed. She sounded melancholy.

"About what?" I asked.

"About Andrew, of course," she said. "His coming home. The first moment, when I saw him, I felt almost wild with joy. His not writing or telephoning, I thought, that was just because he wanted to give us a lovely surprise. But then when Sonia and David began to act as they did, I began to wonder . . . I mean, it couldn't be because he wanted to upset things, could it?"

"You know him much better than I do," I said. "Is it the kind of thing he might do?"

"No," she said. "No, of course not. I know I'm being stupid. I think perhaps it's just that I'm very tired. There's been a lot to do in the last few days. I think I'll take a sleeping-pill tonight to make sure I can cope with things tomorrow. But you know Sonia and Andrew were once engaged to be married."

"So Felix was telling me. He knew them all quite well at one time."

"Yes, of course. And it was Sonia who particularly wanted us to ask Felix to be here. She's always been fond of him. I suppose there really isn't any hope, Virginia, that you and he . . . No, I know you don't like me saying that kind of thing. But why shouldn't Sonia and David be as friendly to Andrew as you and Felix are to one another?"

"Perhaps they will be tomorrow when they've got used to the idea of his being here."

"Is that what you really think?"

Before my talk with Felix I would probably have said that it was. Now I hesitated and she took me up quickly.

"You don't, do you? You think he may try to get Sonia to go away with him before she finally commits herself."

"But doesn't he know she's been living with David for some time?" I asked. "I thought most people knew that."

"I don't know what he knows. Remember he's been away in America for a long time and I don't suppose she's been writing to him. All the same, I'm sure you're right, he must know about it. Paul might have told him. They were always very good friends. They were all such good friends once, the kind you make about the time when you're at a university, perhaps when you've only met two or three times, yet something happens somehow and the friendships last for the rest of your lives. I was never at a university myself. I was at drama school. Yet I've one or two friends from those days whom I still see from time to time and even if it's several years since we last met we always feel it was only the other day. There were those three boys—I mean Andrew and David and Paul—and there was Sonia and another girl whose name I don't remember and I don't know what happened to her. I think she faded out. But I know I thought the others would always be friends. But then there was the trouble about Andrew's and Sonia's marriage, and he went abroad and became successful and wouldn't come home, and she began her thing with David. . . ." She paused, giving a deep sigh. "It's such an awful thing to say, but I wish Andrew hadn't come. They hate him, don't they?"

"Hate's a pretty strong word," I said. "I don't believe many people actually hate one another."

"That's only because you don't yourself," she said. "It's the way you're made. But don't you hate horrible dictators who torture and kill people, and hooligans who ruin other people's enjoyment for them and may even kill a few and go looting and rioting, and IRA murderers who plant bombs and do unspeakable things?"

"Oh yes, but it's so easy to hate people on television when one hasn't got to take responsibility for one's hatred. Face to face its different. I don't believe I've ever known anyone personally whom it was worth hating. It's much harder than loving."

She stood up.

"I suppose I agree with you," she said. "I've never come near to hating anyone enough to feel for instance that I'd like to murder them, yet I've known a few people for whom I believe I'd be willing to give up my own life. Perhaps I wouldn't really. I may be much too much of a coward, but I can at least imagine it. Good-night, Virginia. You'll help tomorrow, won't you, if you see anything going wrong?"

"I'll do anything I can," I promised.

But as it turned out, there was nothing that I could do.

I went to bed as soon as Christine left me, and read an Eric Ambler for some time that I found on a bookshelf in the room. Then I slept soundly till nearly half-past seven, when Ilse came plunging suddenly into my room. I thought for a moment that she must be bringing me morning tea, but then saw that she had no tea-tray and also that if she had been carrying one she could not possibly have come leaping in as she did.

Her face was very pale.

"Please!" she gasped. "Please, Mrs. Freer, you are to come at once."

"Come where, Ilse?" I sat up quickly.

"To the bungalow. Mr. Freer . . . Oh, I was so frightened, Mrs. Freer. I have never before seen a dead person."

Four _____

FOR A DIZZY MOMENT of shock I thought that she meant that Felix was dead. Then, as I tumbled into my dressing-gown, it came to me that she might have meant that Felix had sent her to fetch me, but she had not been able to get the words out. Someone was dead, and if it was someone whom Felix knew, then it was almost certainly Andrew Appleyard, with whom he had shared the bungalow. I went running down the stairs after Ilse.

At the bottom Mrs. Grantly and Martha were standing, waiting for her to bring someone down, though they might not have expected me, but rather some member of the family. They both looked pale but excited.

"Oh, Mrs. Freer!" Mrs. Grantly exclaimed. "Isn't it terrible?"

As I did not yet know what it was, though I was ready to believe that probably it was terrible, I did not stay to discuss it with her, but ran out after Ilse to the bungalow. It was reached by the door at the end of a passage leading out of the hall and which opened into the courtyard at the back of the house. The bungalow was a small white building with a roof of red pantiles that had been built only about ten years ago. I knew that it contained two bedrooms, each with its own small bathroom, and a space between them not much bigger than a cupboard where there was a small sink, a refrigerator, an electric kettle, and some glass and crockery, so that guests could make drinks or tea and coffee for themselves if they chose. Felix was standing in the entrance to the bungalow, which led straight into this little kitchen.

He put an arm round me, kissed me, and said, "It isn't nice."

"For heaven's sake, what isn't?" I retorted. "What's happened?"

"Hasn't Ilse told you?"

"She only told me she's never seen a dead person before," I said. "I wasn't sure it wasn't you. And Mrs. Grantly said it's terrible."

"So it is, though it all looks quite peaceful. Poor old Andrew. And last night none of us guessed."

"So it's Andrew who's dead, is it?" I said.

"Yes," he replied.

"And what didn't we guess?"

"Why he really came here yesterday."

"Well, why did he?"

"To kill himself. He wanted to see his parents once more before he did it. You'd better come in."

"Have I got to?"

"I think you'd better." He put an arm through mine and drew me in. Ilse by now had vanished back into the house. "I think you're the best person to go and tell George and Christine what's happened."

"So that's what you wanted me for," I said.

"Well, naturally."

It was natural, I knew, for him to expect me to undertake the really distressing thing that certainly had to be done, although he could be right that I was the right person to do it. But being the right person to do a distressing thing, however convinced one may feel that it is obviously one's duty, can be very upsetting.

"All right, let me see him," I said, trying to sound calm though I was shaking.

We went into the bedroom to the right of the entrance where Felix had been waiting. The room was small, with a french window like the one in the room where Felix had slept and in which I had once slept myself and which I knew opened on to a sweep of lawn. Both rooms had red curtains and those here were still drawn so that the room was filled with a dull reddish light. There was a bed in it, a built-in hanging-cupboard and dressing-table, and a small table beside an easy chair, and there were a lamp, a glass, an empty brandy bottle, and an empty pill-bottle on the little table. Andrew's suitcase, only half-unpacked, was on the floor. Andrew's body was slumped in the chair, his head leaning back and looking not uncomfortable. He was fully dressed.

"But why . . . ?" I began, then paused, because there was not much chance that Felix could explain anything to me. But the red light in the room seemed to add something unnecessarily macabre to the scene and I went to the window to draw the curtains back.

Felix stopped me. "Don't touch anything. We'll have to get George and Christine and they'll have to get their doctor and I suppose he'll get the police."

I let my hand fall. "I suppose he will. But there's no question that it's suicide, is there?"

"I shouldn't think so. He left a letter."

He pointed to the little table by the chair. Spread out on it between the glass and the brandy bottle, there was a sheet of paper with writing on it. There was light enough in the room for me to read it.

"My dear Father and Mother. Forgive me for doing

this. I felt I had to see you once more before I did, but the truth is, I wouldn't have very long to live even if I tried to face what would be left of my life. I think this is a better way out than getting crippled, stuck in a wheel chair, and being a burden to everyone. I know you'd look after me, but I couldn't face it. I got the pills from the lab at Arne Webster yesterday afternoon before I came here, so no one need wonder where they came from. All my love to you both and please, please forgive me for the trouble it's bound to cause you. My best wishes to Sonia and David. They deserve happiness. It's something I've never had except when I was a child. Because of you I had a very happy childhood. Perhaps it's my own fault that I've never known it since. But tell Sonia that what I'm doing has nothing to do with her. I've thought this over very carefully and I'm sure I'm doing the right thing. Please forgive me and love me in spite of everything. Andrew."

I could feel tears pricking in my eyes though I had hardly known the man.

"But what was wrong with him?" I said. "Why didn't he say?"

"There'll be a post mortem," Felix said. "They'll find out then."

"It could have been something like multiple sclerosis, I suppose."

"Quite likely. It does hit young people."

"How did you find him this morning?"

"Ilse fetched me in. She brought me some tea and had another tray ready to take in to him, and only a moment after she'd left me she gave an awful scream and came tearing back into the room, saying would I come at once. So I came and saw . . ." He gestured at the figure in the chair.

"You saw the letter at once?"

"Oh yes."

"And now I've got to go and tell George and Christine about it. All right, I'll go. But you know, yesterday he seemed so healthy and normal, didn't he? You couldn't have guessed there was anything wrong with him."

"Not with him. Only about the way Sonia and David reacted to him."

"That might have made him very angry, but hardly suicidal. And wouldn't have reduced him to a wheel chair. No, poor Andrew, if it was one of those awful slow crippling diseases, one can understand that he couldn't face it. I'll go now."

I was glad enough to leave the room, yet of course dreaded what was in front of me.

When I went into the house I found Mrs. Grantly still in the hall, though Martha seemed to be busy laying the table for breakfast in the dining-room. I wondered if anyone would be able to eat it, though I should not have been sorry for some coffee then myself.

"It's true then, is it, Mrs. Freer?" Mrs. Grantly said. "He's really dead?"

"I'm afraid so," I said.

"His heart, was it, or a stroke?"

I was not sure if I ought to tell her what had really happened.

"They'll have to get the doctor to find out," I said.

"Dr. Burrows," she said. "And there'll be a post mortem and an inquest and all, won't there, as Dr. Burrows can't ever have seen him before. He's only been in Allingford two years." There was a trace of relish in her tone. "There had to be a post mortem and an inquest when my poor husband passed on. It was what they call an aneurism. Fit as a fiddle one day, driving his van—he drove a van for a laundry—and in the evening he sat down in his chair to drink the glass of beer he always liked when he got in, and before he'd even reached for the glass he was dead. But then he was fifty-three. Mr. Appleyard wouldn't have been more than thirty, would he?"

I suppose I could have cut her short and pushed past her up the stairs, but I was not sorry to be delayed.

"I don't think so," I said, then took my courage in my hands and went upstairs. On the whole I was glad to hear that Dr. Burrows was the family doctor. I knew him slightly. He was a brisk, competent young man who took most things calmly, even tragedies, though without being callous.

I had only reached the landing above when the door of the bedroom that was next to mine opened and Sonia came out. She was in a dressing-gown and carrying a towel and was obviously on her way to the bathroom. She took one look at me and said immediately, "Whatever's wrong, Virginia?"

I suppose my face showed that I was still in a state of shock. But I felt a cowardly relief at meeting her. To tell her what had happened did not seem as difficult as it would have been to tell Andrew's parents, particularly Christine, and now I could leave that to her. In fact, I wondered why I had not thought of going to her anyway.

"It's Andrew," I said. "He's—he's done something terrible, Sonia. I was on my way to tell George and Christine about it."

She went very still and her eyes suddenly seemed to become very large.

"What's he done?" she asked almost in a whisper.

"He seems to have taken an overdose of sleeping-pills," I said. "He's—he's dead, Sonia. Ilse found him and fetched Felix and he sent for me. And there's a letter saying—well, half-saying why he did it."

She grasped my arm. "He's dead? You're absolutely sure? He's really dead?"

"I'm afraid there isn't any doubt of it," I said, "but of course you'll have to get your doctor."

"And he did it himself?"

"Yes, as I said, he left a letter, explaining it."

"But it wasn't—it can't have had anything to do with me and David."

"I don't think it was. He seems to have found out that he'd got some illness, something that was going to paralyze him, that's how it sounds from what he wrote, and he couldn't face it, and he came home because he wanted to see his parents once more before he did it."

"I don't believe it!" she said.

"Well, you can read his letter yourself."

"He didn't say what the illness was?"

"Not in so many words."

"I don't believe it. I don't think there was anything wrong with him."

"Then why did he do it?"

"To punish me! To do what he could to ruin my life."

She spun round, darted back into her room, and slammed the door.

So after all I was going to have to break the news to George and Christine. But I felt that I was getting my hand in at breaking bad news and I was not as scared of it as I had been a few minutes before.

I tapped at their door and heard Christine call, "Come in."

George was still in bed and appeared to be asleep when I entered, but Christine was sitting at the dressing-table, wearing a dressing-gown, and brushing her hair.

"Oh," she said, "Virginia. I thought you were Ilse with

our tea. She always brings us our tea. Nothing's happened to her, has it?"

"Not to Ilse, no," I said, and would have gone on but she interrupted me.

"I sometimes get worried about that child. I'm not sure if I'm looking after her as I ought. She's really very nervous and excitable. Fran says she's always like that and it's nothing to worry about. They became great friends when Fran stayed with her family in Zurich, you know. But why are you up and about already? Didn't she bring you your tea either? There must be something wrong with her."

"Well, perhaps there is now, though that isn't what I came to tell you," I said. "She took tea in to Felix and Andrew and then—then Felix sent for me because—Christine, I'm just going to tell you this baldly, because I don't know how else to do it. Felix found Andrew dead. It seems last night he took an overdose of sleeping-pills."

It was not astonishing that I was met by silence. Christine simply stared at me. Then it was George who spoke. I had not noticed it but his eyes had opened while Christine had been talking. Probably he had not really been asleep when I came into the room.

He sat up now and said sharply, "Dead? Do you know what you're saying, Virginia?"

"I'm afraid I do," I said. "There isn't any doubt of it."

"An overdose of pills? What pills?"

"I don't know, except that he said he got them from a lab at Arne Webster."

"What do you mean, he said?"

"In a letter he's left for you and Christine. Felix and I have read it. It's just lying there on a table. It isn't anything we opened."

He began scrambling out of bed. He was wearing blue-and-white-striped pyjamas. Reaching for a dressing-gown, he struggled into it, then went to Christine and put a hand on her shoulder.

"Come," he said. "We've got to go and see what's happened."

She was still holding her hairbrush, though she had stopped brushing her hair and was sitting quite still, her thin body rigid. Her face had turned grey. Abruptly she put the brush down, stood up, and swept past me out of the room. George followed her, though as he reached me and gave me his usual startled sort of look, as if he could not think what I was doing there, he muttered something about being sorry for what I had gone through. He was always a considerate man, even at a time of crisis.

I followed them down the stairs and back to the bungalow. Christine was the first to reach it. As I came into the bedroom behind her and George, I saw her snatch up one of Andrew's hands, then let it go as if it had burnt her.

"He's cold, he's dead cold!" she cried. "And stiff! Oh, Andrew, my darling! He's been dead for hours."

"I'm afraid so," Felix said. He was standing by the window. George also went to the dead body of his son and touched his cheek gently. Then he turned sharply to the window and drew back the red curtains, letting in the ordinary daylight. Felix did not try to stop him as he had me. It made the room less eerie. The french window was closed and the lawn beyond it sloped down to a copse of beech trees. The sky was a clear blue with a few puffs of white cloud drifting across it. A faint breeze stirred the leaves of the beeches.

"How did you find this out?" George asked Felix.

Felix told him what he had told me about being frantically summoned by Ilse. Then he pointed to the letter on the table by the chair. It did not seem to occur to George that nothing in the room should be touched, for he picked the letter up and, holding it at arm's length, for it was evident that he had forgotten to bring his reading-glasses, he read it quickly, then handed it to Christine.

"My God, to think that when he was with us last night he was intending . . ." he began, then paused. "But he doesn't say what was wrong with him."

Christine had taken the letter from him, read it, then put it back on the table. Tears were beginning to trickle out of her eyes, though she was not sobbing. She seemed passive, almost as if she acquiesced in what had happened.

"Ah, why didn't he tell us?" she said in a low voice. "Perhaps we could have done something."

"We must get Burrows," George said. "I'll go and phone him."

She caught at his arm. "No, don't go. Don't leave me here. Felix, will you go? There's a book with telephone numbers by the telephone in the hall. You'll find Dr. Burrows' number there."

"There's something just a little odd that I think I ought to point out to you before I go," he said. "I can't make any sense of it myself." He went to the dressing-table. "Look, he left a second letter here."

I had not noticed it before myself. It was only a half sheet of paper. George picked it up and as he had with the other letter, held it at arm's length, and read it with a frown.

"Odd," he said. "Yes, distinctly odd."

He handed it to Christine.

It seemed to precipitate the flood of tears that had been on the edge of coming ever since she had come into the room. She held the letter out to Felix to take back and dropped on to the bed, hiding her face in her hands while her whole body began to tremble.

Felix quietly handed the letter to me.

It said, "I can't help it, I had to do this. Sonia doesn't love me. I saw it in her eyes that evening. I've never really had a chance. What happened before would always be between us. This is the quickest way to put an end to everything. I'm sorry for the trouble it will cause."

The letter ended there without any signature. But one of the odd things about it was that it had been written with a black ballpoint, whereas the letter that had been on the table by the chair was written in blue. Not that that really struck me at the time.

"And there's another peculiar thing," Felix said. He had turned to the chair in which Andrew's body lolled, and pointed at something that I had not noticed before which was on his lap. It was a block of note paper and it had a few lines written on the top page. The paper was the same as that of the letter on the dressing-table and, like it, was written in black.

Stooping over him without touching the block, I read the few lines. They were the same as the beginning of the letter on the dressing-table.

"I can't help it, I had to do this. Sonia doesn't love me. I saw it in her eyes. . . ."

There they stopped. I moved away so that George could read them. He put out a hand to take the block, then had second thoughts and did not touch it. But without his glasses he could not read it where it was.

"Christine," he said, "please take a look at this."

She gave a deep sigh, stood up, and read the couple of lines on the pad. Then she gave a wild gasp.

"That isn't his writing!" she cried. "It's nothing like it!"

Five

DR. BURROWS arrived about half an hour later. Felix and I had gone back into the house, leaving George and Christine alone with their dead, as this was what they had seemed to want. Dr. Burrows came to the front door and Felix brought him in, took him through to the bungalow, then returned to the dining-room, where Ilse, in her long, full-skirted dress and green plastic ear-rings, was pouring out coffee. There were corn flakes on the table and Martha had made some toast, but neither Felix nor I had much inclination to eat.

"So sad," Ilse said, spreading butter and marmalade on some toast for herself and munching it eagerly. "There will be no wedding."

Until that moment I had forgotten the wedding.

"No," I said, "I suppose not."

"Everything will be stopped," she said.

That made sense, though I wondered how it was going to be done. Sonia solved that problem. She came downstairs a few minutes after the doctor had arrived, picked up the telephone in the hall, and from the dining-room we heard her calling The Barley Mow. A minute or two later she came into the room. She was in a shirt and jeans, her hair tied back in a pony-tail with a black ribbon. Her face was drawn, almost wrinkled, as if she had aged by at least ten years since I had seen her last. But she seemed more composed than when we had met upstairs.

"I've just spoken to David, telling him we've got to put everything off," she said. "He agreed that it was the only thing to do. Some coffee, please, Ilse."

Ilse poured out coffee for her and Sonia sat down at the table, but she shook her head when Ilse thrust the corn flakes towards her.

"I'll have to start phoning everyone, telling them not to come," Sonia went on. "I hope no one's started from home already."

She sounded as if she were about to cancel a tennis party because of a shower of rain. I wondered if some of the talent for acting that I had been told existed in the family had descended to her, or if this calm of hers was genuine and she really did not care much about Andrew's death, now that she had had a little time to get used to the thought of it.

"I suppose Fran doesn't know anything about this yet," Felix said.

"Fran?" Sonia said in a tone of surprise, as if until that moment she had forgotten her existence. "No, probably not. She sleeps like a log."

"Then shouldn't you perhaps go up and tell her?" Felix suggested.

"Ilse, will you please do that?" Sonia said. "I've got to start telephoning in a moment."

Ilse looked dismayed, but after a slight hesitation shot out of the room and we heard her running up the stairs.

Sonia turned a hard stare on me.

"You're quite sure of what you told me, are you?" she said. "There can't possibly have been any mistake?"

"If you're asking am I sure that Andrew's dead," I said, "yes, there's no question of it."

"I meant about the letter he left behind."

"There's a letter which says quite plainly he's going to take an overdose of pills because he's got some fearful incurable illness that he can't face." I nearly told her that there was another letter too that gave a quite different reason for what he was going to do, and also about the strange fragment on his lap which began in the same words as that second letter, but which Christine had said was not in his writing. But something stopped me. I could leave that, I thought, to George and Christine.

"Please forget what I said upstairs when you first told me what had happened," Sonia said calmly. "It was only shock. I was very upset by Andrew's coming yesterday. I'd hardly slept and I felt sure he'd try to do something to spoil things today. But I hardly think he'd have gone as far as committing suicide to do it. For one thing, he'd have wanted to be here to watch the effect of what he'd done. It wouldn't have been so much fun for him without that. I suppose the medicals will be able to find out what was wrong with him."

There was a sudden rush of footsteps down the stairs and Fran burst into the room. She was in a dressing-gown with nothing under it, and she looked wet, as if Ilse had caught her in a bath or under a shower.

"Sonia, is it true?" she cried. "Andrew's dead?"

"You'd better get Felix and Virginia to tell you about it," Sonia said, finishing her coffee and standing up. "They've been in his room and seen him. Now I've got to do some telephoning. The wedding's off, naturally, and I've got to stop people coming."

She went out into the hall and I heard the tinkle of the telephone as she dialled.

Fran looked wildly from Felix to me and said, "It is true, is it?"

"I'm afraid it is, Fran," I said. "Your parents and the doctor are in the bungalow with him now, but I shouldn't go out there yourself at present. Wait till they come in and tell you about it."

She seemed suddenly to become aware that her dressing-gown was hanging open, showing her naked young body. She clutched it around her.

"But how did he die?" she asked. "What happened?"

"Ilse didn't tell you?"

"No."

I did not blame Ilse, who had now disappeared, probably to the security of the kitchen regions, which she seemed to inhabit as freely as she did the rest of the house.

I reached for more coffee. I felt as if I could spend the rest of the morning drinking it.

"He seems to have killed himself," I said. "He left a letter behind, saying he'd some incurable illness, and he took an overdose of sleeping-pills, which he said he got yesterday afternoon from a lab at Arne Webster, and he drank some brandy with them and—and just quietly went to sleep, I suppose. It could have been worse, Fran. A man like him, so successful, so full of vitality, having to face ending up in a wheel chair, because that's what he said it would come to. . . ." I stopped, because I knew that I was talking only to convince myself, though I knew that it would not quite do so.

"My brother who'd just come home!" she murmured. "I've been having dreams about his coming home for ages. I went to all his films. And now. . . . Really, a wheel chair, you said. Oh, I wish he'd told me. I'd have tried to help."

She turned and ran from the room.

From the hall came another tinkle of the telephone bell as yet another wedding-guest was told not to come.

The telephone, however, was taken over a few minutes later by Dr. Burrows, who telephoned the police. He had come into the house with Christine, while George remained in the bungalow. Dr. Burrows was a short, broad young man with a look of thrusting energy about him, though in fact he was a gentle person whose voice was soft and quiet. He gave me a brief nod of recognition, then admitted that he could do with some coffee.

Christine left us, going up to her room, she said to tell her father what had happened and to get dressed, though I thought that it was really because she needed some time to have the cry in private that was threatening to overpower her now even more than it had in the bungalow.

Dr. Burrows observed, "Very tragic. Strange too. That half-written scrawl on his knee, I don't know what to make of it."

"Mrs. Appleyard says it isn't in her son's handwriting," Felix said.

"I know, but she's in a state of shock," the young doctor said. "She may hardly have known what she was saying. That's a matter for the police, anyway. They'll want to see a guaranteed specimen of his writing."

"There's the longer letter he left," I said.

"Yes," he agreed.

But something about the way he said it made me say, "Is there anything wrong with it?"

"I'm not sure which of the letters you're referring to," he said. "There's one in which he says he's got an incurable disease and can't face it, and one in which he seems to imply that he's killing himself because Miss Capel doesn't love him. That's unusual, you know. I mean, suicides don't usually experiment with different versions of why they're about to kill themselves. Because that's what seems to have happened in this case, isn't it? It's as if he wrote that short unfinished letter, wasn't satisfied with it, and wrote the much longer one about his illness. But he didn't throw away or destroy the first draft. Or it could have been the other way round. He could have written the long, fairly careful letter first, then suddenly felt he'd got to say something more and scrawled the other one. But then he wasn't satisfied with that and sat down and started to rewrite it in his chair, but was overcome by the drug he'd taken only a few moments after beginning it. In any case, unusual. Not the way suicides usually act."

"Mightn't the drug he'd taken have confused him so that he hardly knew what he was doing?" Felix said.

"Possible, of course," the doctor answered. "Anything's possible. There's a first time for everything."

"Do you know what the drug was?" Felix asked.

"The empty pill-bottle is labelled Somnolin. That's a drug produced by Arne Webster. It's a fairly strong sleeping-pill, but taken in prescribed doses it's harmless, though it isn't wise to take it with a tumbler of brandy, or perhaps more than a tumbler. Mrs. Appleyard says he must have brought a bottle with him, because it isn't a kind they happen to have in the house, and the bottle's empty, so we don't know yet how much he drank. A post mortem will tell us. She occasionally takes Somnolin herself that I prescribe for her. In fact, she says she took a pill last night, but that her son certainly didn't get hold of her bottle, because it's in her bathroom, almost full."

"In his longer letter he says he got the pills from a lab at Arne Webster in the afternoon," I said.

"Possible," he said again. "The police will go into that, I suppose. Find out if anyone saw him there, and so on. You saw him yesterday evening, did you?"

"Yes," I said.

"And how did he strike you?"

"Pretty normal, I'd say, though I'd never met him be-fore, so I don't really know what was normal with him."

"He didn't seem to you unwell, or depressed, or in any way strange?"

I shook my head.

"I'm not sure about that," Felix said. "My own impression was that he was extremely angry. He and Eldred—that's the man Miss Capel was marrying and whom I suppose she will marry sometime, even if it's got to be put off today—came near to having an open quarrel. Appleyard walked in, taking everyone by surprise, and expecting, I suppose, to be warmly welcomed, and so he was by his parents and his sister, but Miss Capel and Eldred were certainly chilly and that seems to have got Appleyard pretty furious." He turned to me. "Wouldn't you agree?"

"I think so," I said. "Yes, I think that's right."

"So you think that could have meant that he was already in a state of acute tension when he came," Dr. Burrows said. "In fact, perhaps not entirely normal."

"Oh, I don't know about that," Felix said. "As my wife said, we don't know what was normal with him. Anyway, does one commit suicide because one's lost one's temper? Isn't one more likely to commit murder?"

"For that you need means, motive, and opportunity, don't you? And, of course, a victim. If we'd found Eldred dead . . ." He paused. "I think that's the police," he said.

The police, when they came, turned out to be two men whom I had met before, Sergeant Madden and Constable Baker. I knew Jim Baker quite well, because his wife at one time had been my household help. She was a very good-looking young woman of formidable efficiency who had come in twice a week to clean my house, always far more smartly dressed than I was and who to my great regret had left me to go to some more glamorous kind of work. The sergeant was tall and heavily built with ginger hair which was already beginning to recede from his forehead. He greeted Felix and me with a curt "Good morning," and we remained in the dining-room while the doctor took the two policemen out to the bungalow.

When they had gone I asked Felix, "Well, what did you make of all that?"

"Of what the doctor said?"

"Yes."

He wandered about the room, looking undecided.

"He thinks Christine is wrong about those few lines Andrew seems to have been writing when he died not being in his handwriting," he said.

"Suppose they were by him, then, what does it amount to?"

"A rum situation, certainly, for a suicide. It looks as if he began by writing the longer letter telling George and Christine he was incurably ill, either before or soon after he'd taken the pills and the brandy and put it carefully on the table by his chair. Then, as the pills began to take effect, he either forgot entirely he'd written it, or became somehow confused and dashed off another letter on an odd piece of paper from that block which he happened to have handy, telling what may have been the truth about why he was killing himself. I mean, his realization after seeing Sonia and David together that Sonia really didn't love him any more. And then he went and sat down in the chair and altogether forgot he'd written that second letter and began to write it all over again. But before he'd written more than a line or two he lost consciousness and collapsed and died. The handwriting of those last lines could well have been unlike his usual writing."

"Is that how you think it happened?" I asked.

"I really haven't the faintest idea," Felix answered. "I thought you were asking me what I thought your doctor thinks."

"So you don't think that yourself."

"Well, it doesn't quite explain one or two odd things I noticed, but I suppose the police will sort them out."

"Such as?"

"For one, the change from writing with a blue ballpoint to a black one. But that may mean nothing. I expect you noticed that yourself."

"I did, as a matter of fact. What do you make of it?"

"Doesn't it look as if he had a blue and a black in his pocket, happened to use the blue one when he was still normally conscious, put it back in his pocket, then when he got the urge to write the second letter, already feeling pretty groggy, grabbed the first he found and it happened to be the black one? What other explanation could there be?"

"I don't know. I suppose you're right."

"Now tell me something."

"Yes?"

"The wedding's off, that's correct, isn't it?"

"Oh yes, that's what Sonia's doing at the telephone. She's telling all the guests not to come."

"Then what's going to happen to the wedding-presents?"

That was a question that had not crossed my mind that morning. I thought of the display in the library, and also of the wedding-cake that I was sure had been ordered, and the champagne and the food that a caterer would be bringing in. The caterer at least could be told not to bring his wares, though he would no doubt send in his bill for them.

"I don't suppose anything is going to happen to the presents," I said. "Even if the affair in the church and the celebrations have been cancelled and Sonia and David get married very quietly, the presents will be as welcome then as before."

Felix looked discontented. "If I'd known it was going to be like that I wouldn't have gone to all the trouble of getting my jade dragon. I mean, I could have given them something practical, or some books, or something like that, which would have been perfectly acceptable but didn't have to help make a show among all the other presents."

"I wish I knew where you got the jade dragon," I said.

"Oh, in an antique shop that's started up just round the corner from Little Carbery Street," he answered. "Several new shops have opened up there recently, quite good, some of them."

"It's as near home as that?" I said. "Then you'd better be careful, hadn't you? They're liable to notice it if things of some value tend to be missing whenever a certain one of their local customers has been in."

"I don't know what you're talking about," he said. "That dragon cost quite a lot."

"And you paid for it in solid cash?"

"Certainly."

I did not believe him, but the time when I might have argued about it was long past.

"I think . . ." he began, then paused. "I think perhaps I'll just take a look at it. It's an interesting thing."

"You can't mean you're thinking of pocketing it," I protested. "I know you could probably sell it for quite a bit in Allingford, where you aren't known, but it isn't like you to do that. You generally like giving presents."

"Of course I do, and where you get your ideas about me

from I'll never understand!" he exclaimed. "Sell it in Allingford! Actually I was thinking that if Sonia isn't going
to want it I might give it to you. But honestly, I don't
know why I should think of such a thing in view of the
insults you hurl at me."

However, he had gone to the door and I thought it
might be wise on my part to follow him. Sure enough, he
was making for the library.

There was someone else there, someone I had never
seen before. Oh God, I thought, a wedding-guest who
had left home too early to be stopped from coming by one
of Sonia's telephone calls!

The stranger was a young woman with blonde hair curl-
ing on her shoulders, horn-rimmed spectacles with heavy
mascara on the eyelids behind them, thin, plucked eyebrows and a very vivid lipstick on her full, almost pouting
lips. She was wearing a pink silk suit over a frilly white
blouse and very high-heeled shoes. She gave Felix and me
a startled, incredulous look, as if she could not imagine
what he and I should be doing there, then thrust past us
and darted from the room.

It was only after she had gone that I noticed that the
necklace which George had given Sonia was missing.

Six

FOR A BEWILDERED MOMENT I wondered if by some stroke of magic Felix had managed to slip the necklace into a pocket. But he had been nowhere near it and the stranger had been standing only a foot or two from where it had been.

We both turned and hurried out into the hall. We heard a car start up outside, and as Felix pulled the front door open we saw a battered white Mini disappearing along the drive.

It was only then that I realised that Sonia was not in the hall at the telephone. I looked at Felix.

"We'd better tell the police, hadn't we?" I said.

"Yes," he said, but uncertainly. "The only thing is . . ."

"Well?"

"Hadn't we better wait till they come in? They're rather busy at the moment. But we'll go out and tell them about this if you want to."

Of course I found that I did not want to. I did not want to go back into the bungalow. I did not want to distract Sergeant Madden and Jim Baker in the middle of whatever they were doing. I only rather wished that I could get my own car out of the garage and drive back into Allingford.

But that would be impossible until I was told that I could go.

As we stood in the hall, undecided, Ilse came running down the stairs.

"Oh, where is she?" she gasped. "She is gone?"

"A lady in pink?" I asked.

"Yes, yes, in pink, with *Brillen,* spectacles, and blonde hair. Where is she?"

"Well, I'm afraid she's gone," I said. "Did you let her in, Ilse?"

"Yes, she ring the bell, I open the door, she walk in." She panted a little as if she had just run up the stairs as well as down them. "I say, 'I am sorry, there is no wedding.' She say, 'Which wedding?' I say, 'The wedding of Miss Sonia Capel and Mr. David Eldred.' And she swore. I swear to you, she swore. She used low words I cannot repeat. And she say, 'So it's off, is it?' So I say, 'Of course, because poor Mr. Appleyard is dead.' And she say, very quick, 'Old George Appleyard?' And I say, 'No, no, his son, Mr. Andrew Appleyard, the famous actor. He comes here last night and now he is dead.' And she say, 'But he wasn't going to marry anyone, was he?' And I say, 'No, but to have a fine wedding this morning would not be proper.' And all the time she has not told me who she is. So I think I will tell Miss Capel about her and I run upstairs and I find Miss Capel in her bedroom, lying on her bed and crying as if her heart would break. So I do not know if I should trouble her by telling her about this pink lady. But then she sees me at the door, so I tell her and she shakes her head and says she has never known any such person. So I come downstairs again and find you, and you say the lady has gone."

"So when you let her in, Ilse, you left her here in the

hall, did you?" Felix said. "You didn't show her into the drawing-room or the library?"

"No, I left her just where you are standing," she replied.

"And when you told her that there was to be no wedding today, she said, '*Which* wedding?' Not what wedding, or whose wedding?"

"Ah, I am not sure," she said. "I may have told you wrong. My English, you see, is not yet very good."

"It's excellent," he said kindly. "But perhaps she didn't say, 'Which wedding?' "

I did not know what he was getting at, any more than Ilse did, but I said, "If Sonia didn't know who she might have been, it looks as if she was just some sneak-thief, coming here on the off-chance of getting a chance at the wedding presents."

"I think so myself," Ilse said. "And I left her here alone in the hall, so I am to blame if anything is missing. Oh, I hope nothing is missing!"

"I'm afraid a very pretty necklace is missing," I said. "She had a few minutes to herself in the library before we happened to go in and she must have taken it, but of course you aren't responsible, Ilse. It must have been very difficult for you to know what to do with her. I suppose you thought she was a wedding-guest, arriving rather early."

"Yes, I did at first," she said, "then, I don't know, when she does not tell me her name and when she swore, I think . . . I do not know what I think."

"Now what are we going to do?" Felix said. "Go out and tell the police about it, or wait till they come in?"

But again we did not have to make an immediate decision, because just then Christine appeared on the staircase. She came slowly down with one hand holding tightly on to the banister on one side of it. She was very pale and her eyelids were red and swollen, but her eyes were dry. She was wearing a badly fitting grey skirt and a loose grey jersey and as ever managed to look as elegant in them as she did in her usual jeans, which perhaps she did not feel would be appropriate in a house of death, even if she did not think mourning necessary.

I told her about the strange woman and the missing necklace.

Christine gave a tired shrug of her shoulders.

"It's insured," she said indifferently.

She led the way into the drawing-room and Felix and I followed her. Ilse fled again to the kitchen regions and Christine went to the french window and flung it open, standing there, looking out across the swimming-pool and the garden beyond it with an air of deep sadness, a sadness which wisely she had made up her mind now to let herself experience to the limit.

"It meant so much to me, you know, his coming home," she said. "But after all it didn't really mean much, did it?"

"Christine, we haven't yet told the police about the necklace and all," Felix said. "Shall we do that now"

"Don't interrupt them," she answered. "They'll be coming in presently."

At that moment Sonia came into the room.

"I haven't finished telephoning," she said. "I—I sort of broke down and couldn't go on. I've put most people off, but there are still a few I've got to get through to."

Christine turned back from the french window.

"Sonia, were you expecting anyone with spectacles and blonde hair, who might be given to stealing things?" she asked.

Sonia gave a puzzled frown. "What d'you mean?"

"You tell her," Christine said to me.

"It's just that a short time ago Felix and I went into the library," I said, "and there was a woman there of I should think about thirty, and she was dressed in a pink silk suit and had blonde hair to her shoulders, probably bleached, I think, and glasses, and as soon as she saw us she dashed out of the room and we found then that the necklace George gave you was missing. We can't swear, of course, that the woman took it."

"Who else could have taken it?" Christine asked. "You aren't accusing Mrs. Grantly, or Martha, or Bob, or Ilse, are you?"

"No," I said. "But suppose someone else got in during the night. We don't really know what went on here last night, do we?"

"What do you mean?"

"Nothing," I said, and of course I did not, though with more understanding I might well have done so. "You don't know her, do you, Sonia?"

She shook her head, "Ilse tried to tell me about her, but I don't know anyone as you describe her. Of course some friend of mine may have recently taken to dying her hair and had to take to glasses."

"You see, if she was just a sneak-thief who'd heard there was going to be a wedding here and came in on the chance of being able to pick something up," I said, "wouldn't she have waited till later, when she could be fairly sure you'd all be at the church."

"For God's sake, Virginia, don't be so reasonable!" Christine exclaimed, her voice suddenly changing. "Don't you understand, it doesn't matter? It's such a small thing. We'll tell the police about it presently, of course, but don't let's worry about it now." She turned on Felix. "What are you doing?"

He had taken a small notebook out of a pocket and was jotting something down in it.

"I'm just making a note of the number of the woman's car, before I forget it," he said. It was an old white Mini and I happened to notice the number."

She gave a sigh. "Of course you're right and I'm just being stupid. It can't have anything to do with Andrew and he's all I can think about just now, but I suppose there'll have to be some attempt made to trace the woman, only I can't make myself care in the least about her."

"Christine, would it be best if Felix and I went home?" I asked. "We're just in your way here, aren't we? Shall we go?"

Her gaze on me sharpened at once. "No!" she said. "No, please don't go. You're someone I can talk to. But of course if you want to go . . ." She turned to Sonia. "Oughtn't you to be getting on with that telephoning?"

"Yes, of course." Sonia turned back into the hall. We heard the tinkle of the telephone bell as she started dialling once more.

"You see, I can't talk to Sonia, because she's blaming herself," Christine went on. "Quite wrongly, of course, because it's not her fault if Andrew had multiple sclerosis or whatever it was. But she's sure he really died of a broken heart because of the way she treated him years ago. Vanity of a sort, you could call it, I suppose, and a bit of sheer hysteria. She and I have never got on very well, you know."

This surprised me. I had thought that they had a fairly affectionate relationship.

"I never really forgave her for what she did to Andrew, you see, and she knew that," Christine said. "I know the miscarriage she'd had made her temporarily a bit peculiar, but she recovered from that all right and she could still have patched things up with him before he went away. But she had this thing by then about marriages of first cousins. She blamed it for the miscarriage and for the fact that the baby, if it had lived, would have been a mongol— only you don't call it that any more, do you? It's Down's Syndrome. Probably all nonsense that about they're being first cousins, but it was what she believed—oh dearest," she turned to the door as her father came into the room. "Have you had any breakfast?"

"Yes, thank you," he said, and kissed her and gave a grave nod to Felix and to me.

Fran came into the room too then, dressed again in her bikini, with a loose, flowery pattered shirt hanging loosely over it, and Felix, taking me by the arm, whispered in my ear, "Let's leave the family to themselves. We're no help to them at the moment and I want a talk with Bob."

He drew me out of the room.

I did not know why he wanted to talk to Bob, but that would emerge, I presumed, if we succeeded in finding the young man. We did so almost at once in the garage, where he was very energetically polishing Christine's Jaguar. He did it with frowning intensity, as if expending so much force upon the car would somehow help to keep more upsetting thoughts at bay. He was a comely young man with a fresh, round face, curly brown hair, bright brown eyes, and an expression that looked as if it were meant for smiling friendliness, not distress.

He straightened up as he saw Felix and me approach and said, "Hallo."

"Hallo," Felix said. "You look busy."

"Best thing to be, time like this," Bob said.

"You know about what's happened, then?" Felix asked.

"Can't say that," Bob answered. "Nor can anyone, can

they? Never have been able to understand how a bloke can take his own life. Not unless maybe he was going blind. Dare say I might do it if I knew I was going blind. Yet there's blind people who seem to lead a pretty good life. It's just that I don't think I could face it myself. Couldn't drive, couldn't play cricket, couldn't watch it even on the telly."

"It seems probable Appleyard had some crippling disease that was going to land him in a wheel chair," Felix said.

"Poor chap," Bob said. "Maybe I couldn't face that either."

"But there was something else I wanted to ask you about," Felix went on. "Did you happen to see a woman arrive here in a white Mini this morning?"

"Woman in pink?" Bob asked.

"Yes," Felix said.

"That's right, I did. Someone coming to the wedding, not knowing it was cancelled, wasn't she?"

"Possibly. Did you speak to her?"

"Only a few words. She got out of the car and I went up to her, not knowing if I should put the car in the garage. She'd rung the doorbell by then and was waiting on the step. And as soon as she saw me she said, 'Mr. Eldred and Mr. Camrose are staying here, aren't they?' And I said, 'No, they're staying at The Barley Mow in Oldenham.' And she said, 'I thought they'd be here.' And I said again, 'No.' But just then Ilse opened the door and the woman went inside. Is it important?"

"Probably not," Felix said.

"She only stayed in the house a few minutes," Bob said. "Ilse hadn't even shut the door on her when she came rushing out. Well, I say rushing out, all I mean is, she seemed in a hurry and she jumped in her car and drove off."

"Well, thanks," Felix said.

"Is it important?" Bob asked again with anxiety in his voice.

"It's only that no one seems to know who she is," Felix said. "She didn't tell you her name or anything?"

"Oh no. Wasn't she expected? Perhaps Mr. Eldred can tell you about her when he gets here."

"Yes, we'll ask him."

We returned indoors. I was uneasy, because I felt that Felix's questioning of Bob had had more significance than he wanted to admit, but unless he thought that what he had managed to dig up meant that the woman was some-one out of David Eldred's past who perhaps had come to make trouble at the wedding, I did not know why this should be.

Before we rejoined the others I asked him if that was what was on his mind.

"Not particularly," he answered casually, and I knew from his tone that I should get nothing more out of him.

General Searle was not with the others in the drawing-room, and I guessed that he had gone out to the bunga-low to see if he could be of any use there. Fran was not quite in the room either, for she was sitting in a chair on the terrace just outside the french window, gazing away across the pool as if she was deep in some dream. Sonia, who appeared to have finished her telephoning, was pre-tending to read *The Times*. She kept turning the pages, making them rustle noisily, which made Christine fidget irritably and frown as if she wanted to tell her to stop doing it, but keeping the words back. She was standing in front of the empty fireplace and smoking a cigarette, which was not customary with her, but as if the sight of her doing this reassured Felix that he might do it too, he lit one at once and very soon afterwards lit another. He was normally almost a chain-smoker, feeling that lung cancer, heart disease, and other troubles might afflict other people but would never threaten him. It was only when I saw him with the usual cigarette dangling from his lips that it struck me how rigorously he had controlled himself that morning, refraining as if in respect for the dead.

"I know it's early in the morning for it," Christine said suddenly, "but I'm going to have a drink. Whisky. Anyone join me?"

"I will," I said. I had lost all sense of what time of day it was and anyway what did that matter?

"Sonia?" Christine asked.

"No thanks," Sonia answered. "You know, you'd better send a notice of Andrew's death to *The Times,* hadn't you?"

"I suppose so," Christine said. "And they'll do an obituary of him. And we'll have reporters down here any time now, I should think. I expect it's got around the village that the wedding's off and why it is, and someone will have phoned in to the local paper and so on."

She went quickly out of the room and in a minute or two returned with three glasses, a bottle of whisky, and a bottle of soda water. Without asking Felix if he wanted a drink, she poured one out for him, but when she brought it to him he shook his head. He dislikes whisky and in any case is a very moderate drinker, being afraid, I have always thought, that only a very little too much is liable to make him lose the slender hold he has on reality, and start him telling fictions about himself which would be simply impossible for anyone to swallow. I remember an occasion when, not being even half-way drunk, he had told some companions about his adventures on board a minesweeper during the war, which would have been at a time, as they could easily have calculated, when he was an infant in arms. As a result they had treated him ever after with the gentle deference that is reserved for the definitely crazy, even though, because of his charm, their friendship for him had not much diminished.

I accepted my own drink with gratitude, but I had only just begun on it when I heard footsteps in the hall, and George, the General, and Sergeant Madden came into the room.

"The ambulance has come and gone," George said in a flat, sad tone. "There's got to be a post mortem. Then there'll be an inquest and there's no telling when we can have the funeral. Sergeant Madden has found one or two rather curious things. I don't know if they're important."

"Where's Dr. Burrows?" Christine asked.

"He's gone," George answered. "He left straight after the ambulance. But these things Sergeant Madden found . . ." He paused and looked at the sergeant.

He took it as an invitation to explain. "First there's the fact that we haven't been able to find a blue ballpoint in the room. There's a black one that we found in the chair Mr. Appleyard was sitting in, but no blue, either in his pockets or down the sides of that chair, or rolled under the bed, or anywhere else. Of course there'll be a more thorough search for it later, but so far we haven't found it. And then there's the fact that there's a gun in his suitcase."

"A *gun!*" Christine cried, her voice so shrill that it was almost a scream. "You don't mean that!"

"I'm afraid I do, Mrs. Appleyard," the sergeant answered. "Of course, he'd just come from America and it's easier to get guns there than it is here, and I believe it's more normal to carry them. I've heard of ladies carrying them around as a normal thing in their handbags. How it got through Customs, I don't know. Just by chance, I suppose. And it may not really mean much."

"What could it mean?" Christine demanded.

"Well, nothing, unless he meant to use it."

"What's that in your hand?" Sonia suddenly asked. She had tossed *The Times* aside and stood up.

Sergeant Madden held out the pad of paper that he was holding.

"It's the letter Mr. Appleyard started to write before he dropped off," he said. "The other letters are still where he left them, but we couldn't let his body be moved without taking this." He held it out for Sonia to read. "I don't know if you've seen it yet, Miss Capel."

She went so white and her face looked so strange that I thought that she was going to faint.

"No, it can't be," she said hoarsely. "It's impossible. No, no, that's absolute nonsense."

"Are you all right, my dear?" General Searle asked.

"Yes, I'm all right," she said. "It's just that for a moment . . ."

"Yes?" George said as she stopped.

She drew a deep breath then said very calmly, "After all, I'm afraid it isn't nonsense. You see, that's David's handwriting."

Seven

ONLY A FEW MINUTES LATER David and Paul came in. They had walked up from the village and both had an air of bewilderment and concern, though it showed in them in different ways. In David, who so often had a look of being a little lost and unsure of himself anyway, it gave him an appearance of having strayed into some foreign territory where unfortunately he did not speak the language, while Paul, whose normal self-confidence did not seem much impaired, looked ready to take on some unspecified opponent and make mincemeat of him.

It was Paul who spoke first.

"This is a hell of a thing," he said, "having to put everything off like this at the last minute. For God's sake, I don't mean to say it isn't an awful thing that's happened, but couldn't something have been done—"

"No!" David interrupted with more firmness than I would have expected. "Of course not. Christine—" He put an arm round her and kissed her on one temple. The kiss seemed nearly to miss the spot at which he was aiming, but seemed lovingly meant. "I can't tell you how sorry I am."

"Can you tell us just what happened?" Paul asked. "Sonia didn't say much on the telephone."

"What appears to have happened," George answered, "is that our son Andrew last night took an overdose of Somnolin, a fairly strong sleeping-pill made by Arne Webster, and died in the night."

"Do you mean he did it deliberately, or was it an accident?" Paul asked.

"Oh, deliberately," George said with a kind of fierceness, as if the question angered him. "It was suicide. And he left a letter to Christine and me, saying he was doing it because he'd got some illness that was going to land him in a wheel chair and that he wanted to see us once more before he did it. It's occurred to me that he may have come here to do it because he knew where to go in the Arne Webster lab to get the Somnolin. Paul, you were in their offices here yesterday, weren't you? Did you see him?"

"No," Paul said.

"What about you, David?" George asked.

"No," David said.

"If I may have your attention for a moment, Mr. Eldred," Sergeant Madden said, "is this your handwriting?"

He held out to David the pad of paper that he had brought from the bungalow.

David gave it a glance. "Looks like it," he said. "Yes, only . . ." He started, frowned as he read what was written on the paper and read aloud in a puzzled tone, " 'I can't help it, I had to do this. Sonia doesn't love me. I saw it in her eyes. . . .' I didn't write that!"

"But it's your writing," Sonia said.

"Very like it, anyway," David said, "but I never wrote that. Where does it come from?"

"It was on Mr. Appleyard's lap," Sergeant Madden said.

"When he was dead, do you mean?"

"Yes, his body was in a chair in his room in the bunga- low outside, and this was on his lap," the sergeant replied.

"Then he must have written it himself," David said.

"But why in your writing?" Sonia asked. "For heaven's sake, why?"

"Well, why should I have written a thing like that and left it on his lap when I suppose he was dying?" David had quite lost his abstracted air and looked agitated and ex- cited. His eyes behind his round tinted spectacles seemed to have brightened, so that I felt almost certain that they were blue.

"It must have been just an accident that it looks like my writing."

"You would be prepared to sign a statement then, sir, that you did not write this?" Sergeant Madden asked.

"Certainly!" David answered.

"The strange thing is," George said, "that there are two other letters in Andrew's room, one of which begins in the same words as this but goes on and says a little more, but which is in a quite different handwriting from this, and another in the same writing as that other one and which gives us the facts about his illness."

"Are those two letters in Andrew's handwriting?" Paul asked.

"Oh yes," Christine answered. "There's no doubt of that."

"If I may ask you, Mrs. Appleyard," Sergeant Madden said, "have you a specimen of your son's handwriting which you are absolutely certain was written by him?"

She frowned. "What are you suggesting?"

"Nothing at the moment," he said, "but there seems to be a good deal of confusion about these letters which we ought to clear up. I should like an expert to look at all of them. So if you've a specimen which you can guarantee is authentic, it might be helpful."

"You mean you think someone may have forged those letters?" she said.

"One or both," he replied, "or perhaps neither. It's only that in the circumstances it might be best to explore every avenue."

"Avenues seem to have been invented just to be explored, don't they?" Felix said. "Yet mostly they're such uninteresting places. Acacia Avenue, Myrtle Avenue, that sort of thing. But of course there's a good supply of them in New York which may be more interesting."

Quite properly, no one took any notice of him.

"But who could have forged either of the letters, and why?" Christine asked.

"Have you a genuine specimen of his writing?" the sergeant inquired again.

"I think so, yes." She hesitated. "He wrote very seldom. Mostly it was just Christmas cards and so on. But when he first went out to America he wrote more often and I kept all his letters. If you'll wait a moment . . ." She went out of the room.

Fran just then came in from the terrace.

"I'm going in swimming," she said. "I can't stand it, just sitting there. I've heard all you've been saying and of course it's nonsense. Andrew wrote all those letters. It seems to me quite easy to explain really. If the writing of the bit he was doing when he—when he died—looks like David's, then it must be a sort of psychological thing, I mean, he knew Sonia was in love with David and he wanted to be in David's place and for a little while he even believed he was David and so his writing got like his. Isn't that obvious?"

"It might even be true," David said.

"Sounds absurd to me," the General said. But perhaps generals are not much inclined to be interested in psychology.

"Did he know your writing, David?" George asked.

"He might," David answered. "I suppose I've written to him two or three times since he went away."

"Well, I'm going in swimming," Fran said with a note of defiance in her voice, as if she expected to be told that this would not be proper. "Paul, why don't you come in too?"

He gave her a slight smile. "I would if I could, but my swimming things, and I think David's too, are in Andrew's room and I don't suppose Sergeant Madden would want us to take them out."

"Not just now, if you don't mind," the sergeant said.

Fran turned and went out on to the terrace again. A moment later I heard the splash as she dived into the pool. Christine came back into the room. She held out an envelope to the sergeant.

"This is a letter I had from my son about three years ago," she said. "He wrote that he was thinking of coming home, but he didn't come and we'd only a card to say he'd called the visit off. But you can be absolutely sure this is his genuine handwriting. I'd like the letter back when you've finished with it."

"Of course," the sergeant said. "I'm sorry if this distresses you, as I'm sure it does, Mrs. Appleyard, but I'm sure too you're as anxious as I am to have the whole situation explained. Now may I ask you, did you notice when you were in your son's room that the window was unlatched?"

"No," George said, "I didn't notice."

"Not that it need mean anything on a hot night like last night," the sergeant went on. "He may even have had it open earlier, though it isn't everyone who'd sleep with a french window open on the ground floor."

"If you look in my room," Felix said, "you'll see that my window is open."

"We did look, as a matter of fact," Sergeant Madden said, "and that's why I said it might not mean anything."

"All the same, what you're suggesting, Sergeant," George said, "is that someone could have got into that room last night and planted those letters, aren't you?"

Before the sergeant could answer, and as if she had thought of this possibility herself, Sonia suddenly cried out, "But why? Why? All right, perhaps one or all of them are forgeries, but what was the point of doing it? Has someone here gone mad?"

David put an arm protectively round her.

"Take it easy," he said. "No one's gone mad. There'll be some quite simple explanation of it all."

I did not believe that there would be any simple explanation. Fran's, although a good effort, did not seem to me very plausible. On the other hand, I had nothing to offer myself. It did not particularly help matters, I thought, that Felix chose that moment to tell the sergeant about the missing necklace.

"We've another mystery on our hands just now," he said. "A woman came into the house this morning whom no one seems able to identify. Ilse, the Swiss girl, let her in and left her to herself for a few minutes in the hall while she went upstairs to ask Miss Capel what she should do with her. She assumed, you see, that she was a wedding-guest who hadn't heard that the wedding had been put off. And my wife and I encountered this woman in the library, where all the wedding-presents are set out, and as soon as she saw us she did a bolt and we saw then that a necklace which Mr. Appleyard had given to Miss Capel was missing. And the woman took off fast in a white Mini, and I've got the number of it written down here, if you want it."

He took his notebook out of his pocket.

Sergeant Madden looked round the room. "Does this mean anything to anyone?" he asked.

No one answered.

The sergeant looked back to Felix. "Can you describe her?"

"Age about thirty," Felix said, "medium height, blonde hair, spectacles. Dressed in pink."

"*Blonde* hair?" David said abruptly, sounding as if the description might have meant something if she had not been blonde.

"Might have been a wig," Felix said. "Ask Virginia."

"It could have been a wig," I agreed. "Or at least bleached. It probably was. And as a matter of fact, David, she asked if you were staying here. Were you expecting anyone?"

He shook his head and turned to Paul. "Were you?"

"No," Paul said. "I wasn't involved in asking anyone down for the wedding, was I, Sonia?"

"No, you weren't even here when we made out the list of the people we wanted to ask," she answered. "I think she was just a thief who'd heard there was to be a wedding and thought she might mingle with the real guests without being noticed while she nicked what she could. I know she was a bit early for that, but she may have picked up some misleading information about the actual time the wedding was to be."

"If you'll give me the number of her car," the sergeant said to Felix, "that may be useful." But he did not sound very interested.

Felix handed him his notebook and the sergeant copied the number down into one of his own.

"Constable Baker and I will be leaving now," he said. "We'll leave the room in the bungalow locked for the present, and we'll be taking the other letters with us to show to our expert on forgeries. If there's any possibility that even one was forged, which we can't say is impossible, we'll want them all to be examined. Meanwhile I'd be obliged if you don't try to go into the room. You've no doubt a spare key."

George looked offended. "Certainly no one will go into the room till you tell us you've cleared things up to your satisfaction."

"There goes my hope of a swim," Paul said. He strolled out on to the terrace. "Hi, Fran!" he called out.

She climbed dripping out of the pool and flung herself down on one of the chairs there.

"Unless someone will lend me something to wear, I can't go in," he said.

"I'll lend you my trunks, if they aren't too old-fashioned for you," the General said.

"Will you really?" Paul said. "I'd be immensely grateful. It's a good morning for a swim."

The atmosphere in the room was changing. Some of the tension had gone and with it Sergeant Madden too. General Searle went to fetch his swimming-trunks, and Christine quietly helped herself to a second whisky and another cigarette and sat down on a sofa to brood. George sat down beside her and she leant against him, letting a few tears trickle down her cheeks without attempting to stop them. Sonia and David wandered away together into the garden. Felix muttered something about going to his room, which meant that he was going to the bungalow, which I did not think was altogether wise, and I did not dream of going with him. Even without the use of a spare key he would find no difficulty in entering Andrew's room, if that happened to be what he had in mind, and if so, I did not want to be in on it. I sat down in a chair on the terrace, near to Fran.

After a few minutes Paul appeared, wearing the General's trunks, having apparently changed upstairs, and, going to the spring board at the end of the pool, he did a very perfect dive into the water.

Fran gave a sigh. "Isn't he handsome?" she breathed, as she had the evening before of her brother.

"He is rather," I agreed.

"And he's clever too, so Dad says," she went on. "They're going to move him to the London office. But you know, I think I'm going to ask him to marry me."

"Well, good luck," I said.

"You don't think he'll have me?"

"I don't know anything about it."

"He may not, you know." She did not sound deeply troubled by the thought, and I was not sure how serious she was. "If he wanted me, I think he'd have done something about it already."

"And he hasn't?"

"Not a thing."

"Then perhaps you'd be wise to put it off for a little."

"Only I'm getting so impatient. I think there must be something stopping him, because I'm sure he cares for me. He keeps giving it away in all sorts of ways. Then he just seems to hold back. Actually I think I know what the trouble is, and it's very ridiculous."

"Oh yes?" I said.

"You see, I'm a rich girl."

"I should have thought that might have made you extra attractive."

"Oh, not if you've got scruples, like Paul. He couldn't bear it if people thought he was marrying me for my money."

"But have you really got such a lot of money, Fran?" I asked. "I should have thought George had a good many years of life ahead of him, and it isn't as if you can be sure of inheriting anything from Andrew, can you?"

"From Andrew? Oh, Lord no. I'm sure he always lived up to all those dollars he earned. Anyway, why should he have left me anything? We hardly knew each other and I'm not talking about Dad. I love the old boy, I honestly couldn't ever think of such a thing. No, it just happens I inherited a very nice amount from an old grand aunt of mine. She said that she was leaving it straight to me instead of to Dad, because he'd already got plenty and this way it would save one lot of death duties. And so Paul's afraid to marry me."

"You really think that's what's holding him back?"

"What else could it be?"

I could think of all sorts of things. It just possibly could be that she was only eighteen and Paul was at least ten years older, and pleasant as he might find it to play around with her, he might think of her as a little too much of a child for marriage. Or there might be another woman in his life, the life he lived in London, or he might even be homosexual. Such thoughts naturally cross one's mind nowadays. I doubted if her possession of a fortune could seriously put him off if he was in love with her. But I did not feel like offering advice. If she took her chance and encountered rejection, it might in the long run help her with the difficult business of growing up.

"I'm going in swimming again," she said, and sprang up and made for the diving-board.

A moment later she and Paul were playing some kind of

game in the pool, splashing each other and shouting what sounded like insults at one another. It was almost difficult to remember that only the night before a man had died so near to them. But perhaps Paul did remember it, I thought, and was doing what he could to keep Fran's mind from dwelling on it. Perhaps she was right that he loved her and that if he held back from her it had something to do with the depth of his feeling for her.

Presently Felix came strolling along the terrace and dropped into the chair next to mine. He had an abstracted frown on his face.

After a moment he said, "Why am I the sort of person I am?"

He did not often have attacks of self-questioning, and I had long ago lost my ability to take them seriously when they happened.

"Go to a psychiatrist and find out," I said. "That's what a lot of people do. In your case, of course, it's something to do with having hated your father."

That he had really hated his father was one of the few facts that he had told me about his childhood which I was sure was authentic. There could have been no dissimulation in the tone in which he spoke of him, even though he always claimed with a trace of pride that the man had been a colonel, whereas I had become fairly sure, from incautious remarks dropped now and then, that he had not been more than a sergeant major. In the same way it had become evident to me that the public school to which Felix had asserted that he had been sent had really been the local comprehensive and which he had also hated, though probably not as much as he would have hated the public school if he had been there. An unhappy childhood had undoubtedly had a lot to do with the kind of man that he had become.

"No, no, I don't mean that," he said impatiently. "But why is it that wherever I go things force themselves on my attention that I simply have to go on thinking about, even when I'm really quite bored by them?"

"If you're thinking about that woman who went off with the necklace—"

He interrupted. "Damn that woman! I'm thinking about Martha."

"Why, whatever has she done?" I asked, truly surprised.

"She was in my room, making my bed, when I went in," he said, "and she said to me at once, 'Oh, Mr. Freer, have you got that glass?' So I asked her what glass and she said, 'Oh, don't you know? Then whatever's happened to it?' And it seems that in the little sort of kitchenette in the bungalow between the two bedrooms there have always been four glasses, along with cups and saucers and a kettle and so on, but now there are only two. One of course is in Andrew's room and there are two in their usual place, but one's missing. And that's what I mean when I say why am I the sort of man I am, because there's this insignificant fact and it gets thrust at me instead of at anyone else. She might have told Baker about it, for instance, but she didn't. And the trouble is I can't help feeling it's important."

Eight

FRAN AND PAUL came climbing out of the pool and dropped into chairs near us.

"That was good," Fran said, "I feel much better now. Do you think it was awful of us, Virginia?"

"I don't see that it can make any difference to anybody," I said.

"But to be enjoying ourselves . . . I tell you what," she said, "when I die I'd like people to make a celebration of it and be cheerful and drink a lot and not sit about and mourn."

"That's what most of us think," I said, "but when it comes to the point of course it isn't possible, because the main character is absent and may even be very sorely missed."

"Is he always missed, do you think?" she asked. "Aren't there sometimes people who are glad to have seen the last of him?"

"Oh, of course," I said. "We can't all be beloved by everyone."

"I loved Andrew," she said, "or I thought I did, but just now, while I was swimming, I realised he was a complete stranger to me. When I was a child, before he went away, I had a sort of hero-worship of him. It was marvellous to have such a handsome, clever, older brother. I used to boast about him to my friends. But he never paid much attention to me really. I expect I was just a nuisance to him because sometimes he'd have to take me to parties and things when my parents were afraid of my going by myself, only they couldn't take me, and it must have been fearfully boring for him, putting up with a lot of kids."

"Would you have gone back to Hollywood with him, if he'd asked you again?" Felix asked.

She hesitated for a moment, then said, "No. Even if he'd meant it, I shouldn't have gone. But of course he couldn't have meant it, considering what he had in mind last night."

"In your place, I'd have gone, if he meant it," Paul said. "It would have been a splendid experience. Sad that it couldn't happen."

She looked displeased. "Well, he didn't mean it, so why are we talking about it? But in any case, I shouldn't have gone."

Not so long as she was thinking of asking Paul to marry her, I thought, but he showed no sign of being aware of this complication in her feelings.

"Ah, drinks," he said as Ilse appeared on the terrace, pushing the trolley with glasses and sherry on it. "Good morning, Ilse. How are you today?"

"I feel terrible," she answered in a slightly shaky tone. "I think I go home." She poured out sherry for the four of us, then one for herself, and sat down on one of the chairs there. "As soon as I can, I go home."

"Oh, Ilse, you don't mean that!" Fran exclaimed. "I know things aren't very nice for you here at the moment, but you won't really leave, will you?"

"Everything is always very nice for me here," Ilse answered. "Everyone is very kind to me. But I am responsible for letting that woman in to steal the jewellery, and I am a foreigner and no one knows anything about my morals. Perhaps they think I am—" she paused, thinking deeply about what to say next. "Perhaps they think I am in *cahoots* with her." She brought the idiom out with a slight air of triumph.

"What nonsense," Fran said. "Anyway, they don't know anything much about any of our morals."

"They?" Ilse said. "The police? You see, at once you think of the police. At home I have never been in the hands of the police."

"I don't think you'll suffer much in the hands of Jim Baker," I said, "and even Sergeant Madden seems to be fairly harmless. I don't think you've anything to be afraid of, Ilse."

"Of course not," Fran said, "and I'll miss you so if you go."

"You will really?" A faint smile appeared on Ilse's sombre little face. "Even if that poor man's death should be murder?"

"Murder!" Fran cried.

It struck me that the only person there who did not look startled, as I am sure I did myself, was Felix.

"Whatever made you say that?" Fran asked.

"It is natural to think of such a thing at a time like this," Ilse answered placidly.

"It certainly isn't," Paul said, "unless you've heard something. . . . Have you heard anything, Ilse?"

"No, only what Mrs. Grantly and Martha and Bob are saying," she said. "They all say it is murder, because what else could it be, they say, a gentleman like him? Such a one does not commit suicide."

"They watch too much television," Paul said. "What would a gentleman like him be doing, getting murdered?"

"Ah," she said, sipping her sherry and looking wise, but otherwise offering no answer.

"Well, I'm going to get dressed," Fran said, and, finishing her sherry at a gulp, disappeared through the french window into the drawing-room.

Paul lingered for a moment, looking troubled.

"I shouldn't repeat that kind of thing if I were you, Ilse," he said. "Even if . . ."

"Even if it is true, perhaps," she said.

"That isn't what I was going to say," he said. "I was going to say even if it's what Mrs. Grantly and company have been saying. It won't help the Appleyards, if you care about that at all."

"I care very much," she said.

"Then be a little more careful what you say." He followed Fran into the house.

Ilse looked sadly at Felix and me.

"Now you see why it is better I go home," she said. "I will always say the wrong thing and do the wrong thing and no one will understand me. You want more sherry?"

"No thanks," Felix said. He lit a cigarette. "I wonder what there is to understand. I've a feeling there's something."

"It is only that last night when he go to his room I am in the garden, going for a little walk before I go to bed, and he laugh and he say, 'You are a pretty girl, Ilse, you are wasting yourself on a job like this.' And he say, 'Now if you feel like a drink by and by and you come to see me, we can have a nice evening.' Now is that what you say when you are thinking of killing yourself?"

"I suppose you didn't go," Felix said.

"Certainly not," she answered. "My morals are very careful."

"Splendid. And of course you don't know if anyone else went to have a drink with him."

"I know nothing, I went straight to my bed."

She finished her sherry, stood up, and wheeled the trolley back into the house.

Felix gave a sigh. "You see how it happens. She comes to me to give me that little tit-bit of information. But why me? Why not Christine, why not Sonia, why not the police?"

"Because of the look of insatiable curiosity on your face," I said.

"But you see, it may turn out to be very important."

"Like the missing glass."

"Oh, so you've been thinking about that."

"Well, naturally."

"And what do you make of it?"

Actually I had not been thinking about it much and had made nothing of it. But I have often found that it does not do to ignore the matters that worry Felix. He can be quite indifferent to major things that worry most people, but little things that catch his attention have an awkward way of turning out to be well worth notice.

"I don't know," I said. "Do you think he had a visitor last night whom he had a drink with?"

"It's possible," he said.

"Did you hear anyone come or go?"

"I heard him—I think it was Andrew himself—come out to that kitchenette for something. I thought at the time perhaps it was a drink of water. I thought perhaps he wanted some for swallowing pills, or something like that. Actually I didn't think anything much about it. Then I went to sleep and didn't wake up till Ilse came bursting into my room, saying he was dead."

"So you didn't hear him talking to anyone."

"Oh no. But I'm not sure if I should have, even if there had been anyone there. That bungalow is quite well built. Its walls are pretty solid."

"You think someone else, whose morals are not as careful as Ilse's, may have visited him?"

"Are you thinking of Sonia? She might have wanted a quiet talk with him. I thought of that. But why should she have walked off with a glass?"

"It's obvious you've some idea about it," I said. "Why don't you go on and tell me about it?"

He blew smoke out before him and watched it fade away in the faint breeze before he answered.

"What could have happened," he said, speaking slowly and almost dreamily, "is that someone came to visit him, coming in through that open french window, and he offered whoever it was a drink and went out to the kitchenette to collect two glasses. That would be when I heard him. We found an empty bottle of brandy in that room, didn't we? And he may have had it in his suitcase, or his visitor might have brought it. And they had a drink together and then the visitor left, but didn't want it known that he or she had been there and so took the glass away with him or her, because of course it would have fingerprints on it, and if he'd simply taken it to the kitchenette and washed it, that could have wakened me."

"So you think this person may have had something to do with Andrew's suicide, or are we talking now about his murder?"

"Take your choice."

I thought that he had made his own mind up about which it was and that made me uneasy.

"My own guess is that there were only three glasses there in the first place," I said. "I don't know who last slept in that bungalow, but whoever it was could have smashed a glass accidentally and dropped the pieces in the waste-bin in the kitchenette, and they got thrown out without being noticed when the rooms were tidied, because at the time there wasn't any drama about to make people start asking melodramatic questions."

"That's perfectly possible, of course."

"So why don't you believe it, because you don't, do you?"

He stubbed his cigarette out in the ash-tray on the ground beside his chair and lit another.

"It's just that it all fits together so neatly and I never can believe in that," he said. "Someone comes to visit him and Andrew lets him in at the french window, or perhaps the window is open already, as mine was, and this person just strolls in. And he's brought a bottle of brandy and a good dose of Somnolin with him, and the two settle down to have a drink together. And when Andrew isn't looking, this character pours the Somnolin into Andrew's brandy and he swallows it. I don't know if it would have made the brandy taste foul, but as it's his guest's present, Andrew, who's got good manners, gulps it down and pretty soon starts going into a doze. And the guest quietly leaves and next day we find Andrew dead. It's neat. It's too neat."

"What about finger-prints on the brandy bottle?" I asked.

"If the man brought it with him, he could have been careful not to handle it and it could have been Andrew who poured out their drinks. I'm sure they'll find Andrew's prints on it. Incidentally, I've just said he, but it could just as easily have been she. Actually I've been wondering if it could have been that woman in pink."

"Good heavens, whatever made you think of her?" I asked.

"Oh, I've only been wondering in a vague sort of way,

not very seriously. But her turning up as she did in the morning, mightn't that have been to find out if her job of poisoning had worked?"

"Neither Bob nor Ilse said she asked for Andrew. She asked for David and Paul."

"Asking for Andrew would have been a bit too obvious, wouldn't it? And she'd have known from the air of calamity in the place, and the wedding having been called off, and from what Ilse told her, that things had gone as she planned. And that was partly why she left in such a hurry when she saw us. She didn't want to risk being stopped and questioned about what she was doing there. And she only took the necklace to conceal her real reason for coming. She wants us to think of her as an ordinary thief. But you know, I've got a very queer feeling about that woman."

"If you're right that she's a murderess, that's hardly surprising."

"No, I mean I've got a sort of feeling that I've seen her before somewhere. I've been trying to imagine what she might have looked like if she hadn't had on a blonde wig, or at least had had hair of a different colour, and no spectacles, and I get a sort of tingling sense that I've almost got there, but I can't quite make it out."

"I suppose you wouldn't be quite so obliging as to supply her with a motive."

"There might be all kinds. Suppose she's an actress. Suppose she and Andrew had some sort of professional connection and he somehow played some dirty trick on her. Or suppose she'd been living with him and thought he'd come here to get Sonia back before she married. Or suppose he knew something about her which he could use to ruin her career, or her marriage to someone else, or—oh, there are limitless possibilities with people like them. And she may even have come over with him from America and knew where he was going and so where she could find him. But I tell you what's wrong with this little idea of mine. Again it's too neat. It's too obvious. Things just don't happen like that."

"Particularly since you haven't said a word about the suicide letters," I said. "Suppose she's a forger along with her other abilities, why should she have left three letters?"

"Yes, indeed, why?" Felix said, and closed his eyes, either to be able to think more deeply or to have a little sleep in the warm sunshine.

It was not until late that afternoon that that question of mine was partly answered and even then it was only partly. A few cobwebs clinging to it were cleared away, but the main problem remained. We had had a very silent lunch during which the name of Andrew was not mentioned even once. Yet there was nothing else to talk about, so the result was an enduring and uncomfortable silence that lasted through the cold salmon and salad and the cheese that followed. The caterers, who I suppose would have provided a meal if the wedding had gone ahead, appeared to have been successfully put off. Over coffee General Searle suddenly started talking about the missing necklace, assuring Sonia that he personally would see to it that she had another, because he still had a few pieces of his wife's jewellery which he had kept for Fran, but which Sonia should see so that she could choose something for herself. She did her best to assure him that the necklace, much as of course she regretted its loss, was not of major importance at the moment, and George said that anyway the police would probably trace it soon. I doubted if he was right, but it disposed of the subject for the time being. When the police arrived at about five o'clock, they had nothing to say about the necklace.

It was not Sergeant Madden and Jim Baker who came then, but a man who introduced himself as Detective Superintendent Dawnay, who was accompanied by a Sergeant Wells. The Superintendent was about forty-five, not as tall as one usually expects policemen to be, and so slenderly built that I could not believe that he could be very useful in a punch-up, yet there was an alertness about him, a natural lightness of movement, that can come only from very well-coordinated muscles. He had thick, dark brown hair and skin dark enough to make his singularly pale grey eyes look almost colourless. The sergeant was a big, burly man with rough fair hair, a reddish face, and blunt features which looked as if a punch-up could not spoil them.

Ilse brought the two of them into the drawing-room, looking very nervous as if she thought that they must have come expressly to take her into custody because of her having let the woman in pink into the house. She lingered in the doorway apparently in case they wanted to arrest her on the spot. But the Superintendent addressed himself to George.

"We've some rather curious information for you, Mr. Appleyard," he said. "Perhaps we could talk in private."

"I should like my wife to hear whatever you have to say," George answered.

"Yes, of course," the Superintendent said. "And perhaps there's no real need for privacy, if you wouldn't prefer it yourself. Someone here may have some useful suggestions to make."

He glanced round the room with those strange pale eyes, and it occurred to me that with his dark skin and his lithe carriage, if he had gone to Hollywood, he might have been as convincing a cattle rustler or Mexican bandit as ever Andrew Appleyard had been.

The whole party had assembled in the drawing-room

over tea which Mrs. Grantly had brought in. General Searle, George, Christine, Sonia, Fran, David, Paul, Felix, and I were all there. But only Fran, with the appetite of the young, had helped herself to some of the excellent cake on the tray.

"Would you like a cup of tea, Superintendent?" Christine asked automatically. At any time when she found herself sitting at a tea-tray and someone had come in she would always have asked him immediately if he would like a cup of tea. In her shabby skirt and jersey she was looking as distinguished as ever.

"No, thank you," Superintendent Dawnay said as automatically.

"Then sit down," she said. "Sergeant, would you like a cup of tea?"

"No, thank you," he said. "We had our tea a little while ago."

The two men sat down side by side on a sofa.

"About this information of yours," George said. "It's something important, is it?"

"It may be of the greatest importance," the Superintendent said, "though I can't pretend we understand it. Someone here may be able to help."

"Well?" George said. I had noticed that day that he had somehow assumed authority in the house in a way which was unusual for him. His air of not being quite sure who it was to whom he was talking had faded. I felt that I understood almost for the first time how he had become the successful businessman that he was.

"It concerns the three letters that were found in your son's room," the Superintendent said. "We haven't had much time yet to give them the examination they need, but certain things about them are fairly evident, according to our own expert. The longer letter in which your son said that he was killing himself because he had an incurable illness is definitely a forgery. A clever one, but still, comparing it with the letter from him which Mrs. Appleyard guarantees as genuine, there can be no doubt of it. The shorter letter, which implies that he was killing himself because he had realised that Miss Capel didn't love him, is undoubtedly genuine. And the few lines of writing on the pad which was found on his lap in the chair where he died, and which were in the same words as the beginning of that second letter, look . . ." He paused and glanced round at us all again. "They look as if he himself was trying to forge someone else's writing."

Nine

IT WAS CHRISTINE who broke the silence that followed.

"Then he wasn't ill! If that letter saying he was ill was a forgery, that wasn't why he killed himself!"

"That seems probable," Superintendent Dawnay said.

"And the other letter, the one he really wrote—" Christine broke off and turned suddenly on Sonia, her face pale with fury. "It's all your doing! You broke his heart all those years ago. You killed him!"

Sonia stood up, walked to the french window, and stood there, looking out. None of us could see the expression on her face.

"Of course, even if that one letter was a forgery," the Superintendent went on, "it might have been the truth. Someone may have known about Mr. Appleyard's state of health and thought it better that you should know it than that you should think—well, what you've just said."

"You don't believe that," Christine said.

"It's true I'm not inclined to do so," he answered. "There's the fact that your son had apparently already written that other letter and left it there on the dressing-table, and there's something else. We've been in touch with his doctor in Hollywood. He happened to have the doctor's name and number in a notebook we found in his pocket, and we've been talking to him. He says he saw Mr. Appleyard only a short time ago, a few weeks. He'd had a fall from a horse during some filming they were doing, and he'd cracked a rib. And it was partly due to his excellent state of health, the doctor said, that it mended as soon as it did. We'll know more about it all after the post mortem, but that doctor's prepared to give him a clean bill of health."

"But suppose he *thought* there was something wrong with him," Fran said. "I mean, after a fall. . . . A fall can have all sorts of peculiar effects on one, can't it? Suppose he banged his head on something and that Hollywood person didn't realise it, and the result of it was that he'd become convinced he was mortally ill, even if he wasn't. . . ." Fran's voice faded. Her tendency to believe in the psychological explanation of most puzzling things did not carry her through. "No, you said that letter was a forgery, didn't you? And he'd already written the other, telling the truth. . . ."

Sonia whirled round from the window.

"It wasn't the truth! God knows why he wrote it, if he really did. How sure are you that he wrote it, Mr. Dawnay?"

"Fairly sure," he said, "but of course it will have to be checked."

"And how do you know that he'd *already* written it before the forgery?"

"The fact is, we don't. It's only that it would be rather strange if he left a forged letter lying on the table beside his chair, and that he then got up and wrote the other letter without thinking of disposing of the forgery."

"So you think someone came into that room when he was already dead or at least unconscious, put the forged letter by his chair, and didn't notice the other on the dressing-table."

"It's one explanation of the circumstances," he said.

"Only I don't believe it!"

She swung round again to the window and strode out on to the terrace.

David hesitated, looked questioningly at the Superintendent as if to see if there was any objection to his following her out, saw no expression on the detective's face, and went out after her. I saw him put his arm round her shoulders, then the two of them wander off into the garden.

"Of course, what you're telling us," Felix observed, "is that you believe the poor chap's death was murder."

The doorbell rang.

Ilse ran out of the room to answer it and a moment later returned, looking awestruck.

"Please, it is the press, Mr. Appleyard," she said, addressing George. "It is television. They say they hear Jon Sanchez is dead. They desire an interview. They desire to take photographs."

General Searle got to his feet rather more rapidly than was his wont.

"I'll deal with this, George," he said. "And mind, all of you, even if I have to let them into the house, not a word about murder. Not a word about forgeries. Don't you agree, Mr. Dawnay?"

"Certainly," the Superintendent said.

The General turned on Felix. "You understand that, do you? I don't know what idiot idea you've got in your head, but keep it to yourself."

He strode out of the room.

He managed to keep the press at bay for some time and eventually got rid of them without having to let them into the house, but the knowledge that they were there seemed to inhibit any further discussion in the drawing-room. We sat there in silence. The Superintendent and the sergeant did not leave until after they had gone, then when the General returned to the room they got to their feet, said that they would let Mr. and Mrs. Appleyard know of any developments, such as the result of the post mortem, and took their leave.

The General gave a sad sort of smile.

"You'll see me on the television news this evening," he said. "I did my best to convey the impression that Andrew died suddenly, probably as the after-effect of a fall he had some weeks ago, and that there's nothing mysterious about it. I believe we shall be told that he was one of the outstanding actors of his generation, which, alas, he wasn't, but I don't think we shall hear so very much more about it."

"Thanks, that's a relief," George said. "Now, Felix, will you tell us what you meant when you said that policeman believes Andrew's death was murder?"

But Felix did not seem inclined to explain what he had meant. He dodged the question by saying that he thought it was what Dawnay had been leading up to because of course he had to explore all those avenues that we had talked about, and the Appleyards gave up trying to get more out of him. But I saw Paul give Felix a long, thoughtful look as if he were storing up questions to put to him at some later, more convenient time. Fran suddenly threw herself into her mother's arms and began to sob helplessly, like a child. Christine looked startled for a moment, then thrust her away from her with a strange gesture of violence. George drew Fran into his arms, kissed her forehead, and began to stroke her hair, as he might have done if she had been only ten years old.

Felix and I, without discussing the matter, chose that

time to stroll out together into the garden. We walked in silence for some way along a wide grass pathway between two luxuriant herbaceous borders where lilies, peonies, poppies, and lupins, as well as more exotic things, were in bloom. Then at last I said, "Well?"

"Well, all right," Felix said. "I know what you want. Was it murder? And is that what the police think it was?"

"And is it?"

"I shouldn't be surprised."

"Can you explain that to me?"

"I'd have thought you'd have seen it for yourself," he said.

"Suppose I have," I said. "Let's suppose someone came with a forged letter prepared, and armed with Somnolin and a bottle of brandy, and with intent to induce Andrew to take an overdose and kill him. But what this character didn't know was that Andrew actually intended to kill himself that evening and had written a letter explaining that he was doing it because of his broken heart. Perhaps Fran's right that his fall and a bump on the head had something to do with it, but anyway, that's the genuine letter that he left on the dressing-table. However, he let this other person into his room to have a final drink with him before he did it, and he swallowed a lot of Somnolin in his drink and died before he could get around to finishing himself off in the way he intended. And his friend left the prepared letter on that little table and cleared off. Is that how it happened?"

"How did Andrew mean to kill himself?" Felix asked.

"He'd a gun in his suitcase, hadn't he?"

"Yes, but there are one or two complicating things you haven't mentioned."

"Meaning?"

"To begin with, that forged letter about Andrew's imaginary illness would have taken a little preparing. I don't imagine you can dash off a forgery like that in a few minutes. To make an artistic job of it would have taken a fair time. And whoever wrote it would have had to know where and when to find Andrew alone and ready for a drink. However, suppose he comes along, they have their drink together, the friend thinks Andrew has had enough Somnolin to be finished off, wants to leave the letter and go. But would he have dared to do that until Andrew was pretty far gone? So did he sit there, watching Andrew doze off and incidentally beginning to write that mysterious letter in David's writing? Or did he perhaps go away before that happened without leaving his own letter and then come back later and leave it? In other words, did he come to the bungalow twice?"

"Is that what you think he did?"

"It's what could have happened."

"And whom are we talking about?"

He did not answer. We strolled on till we came to a gate that opened into the park that surrounded the house and garden. There were massive chestnuts there, and in the little clouds in the pale blue sky above there were flecks of pink as the sun moved towards setting.

"Someone," Felix said after a while as he had said before, "who knew where and when Andrew was to be found that evening."

"That means one of the family."

"Or David, or Paul."

"You've given up your theory that it could have been that woman who pinched the necklace."

"Not really. If Andrew communicated with her somehow, telling her that he'd be in the bungalow, if she'd followed him to Allingford, or perhaps even arrived there with him and he'd telephoned her, wherever she was staying, and told her when to come and see him . . . I admit we don't know that he telephoned anyone, but there are several extensions in that house and he might have been able to do it without anyone overhearing." He paused. "Really I only like it because I hate to think it might have been any of the Appleyards."

"Particularly Sonia."

"She's got the best motive, hasn't she?"

"One of those awful love-hate things?"

"Yes, and last night I think it was all hatred. She'd worked hard at building up her life with David and she thought Andrew had come to try to wreck it. She made that plain enough, and perhaps it was what he meant to do."

"But she'd only to tell him to clear off," I said. "She didn't have to murder him."

"Oh, I know that's how you'd have handled it yourself," he said drily. "Murder can be a kind of compliment. If you really have to kill someone because it's the only way you can get him out of your system, it means you must have cared for him a great deal at one time. But I can't see you ever being driven to it."

"So you think Sonia is a bit insane."

"That's one way of putting it. That rather stiff, satirical manner of hers, with the occasional explosions of hysteria —that adds up to something or other, doesn't it?"

"Where did she get the Somnolin?"

"Perhaps she's been on the stuff herself and happened to have a bottle of it handy."

"Which will be missing now, if she emptied it into Andrew's brandy."

"That's right."

"Well, let's try someone else for size. Suppose we consider David's possibilities as a suspect."

We had come to a bench under one of the chestnuts and both of us turned towards it and sat down there. There were some old nuts from last year lying split open and shrivelled on the ground at our feet, and there was a faint coolness in the air, which made me think that soon we ought to be returning to the house. But it felt very peaceful in the park, away from the turmoil of other people's fears and sorrows.

"I suppose he's got the best motive that we know of," Felix said. "Don't you think so?"

"Because he believed that Andrew would succeed in breaking up his marriage to Sonia."

"Yes."

"Do you think he would have?"

"How's one to tell?"

"I believe you do think so."

"Assuming Sonia's really as unstable as I think she is, why not?"

"Of course he could have got the Somnolin easily at Arne Webster."

"Yes."

"And he knew that Andrew would be in the bungalow, and he probably could have persuaded him to let him in and have a drink while they had a discussion of the wedding next day and what it was going to mean to them both. And he and Paul both had keys to The Barley Mow, so he could have come and gone from it without anyone knowing. So that's means, motive, and opportunity. But I know what you'll say about it. You'll say it's too neat."

"There's something about it that isn't at all neat," Felix said, "and that's those few lines in David's writing on Andrew's lap. And there's the fact that he'd have had to come and go twice. Not that that necessarily means anything. He could have wandered out here where no one was likely

to see him late in the evening, and waited until the medi-
cation had had time to work."

I had a sudden sense that that was what must have happened and that Felix and I were now sitting there comfort-
ably in the pleasant evening where the night before a murderer had sat and waited for his victim to die. It was not an
agreeable feeling.

"Well, what about Paul?" I said.

"Ah yes, Paul."

"Why do you say, 'Ah yes, Paul,' in that way?" I asked.

"I wasn't aware that I said it in any particular way," Felix
answered. "But naturally I've been thinking about him.
He'd means and opportunity, just like David, but what
about motive? Have you any ideas about that?"

"Not really, no."

"You mean you have."

I shook my head. "It's just that I was remembering a
chat I had with Fran this morning. She told me she
thought Paul's in love with her but won't do anything
about it because he couldn't bear it if people thought he
was marrying her for her money. It seems a grand aunt left
her money and she's quite rich, apart from anything she
may eventually inherit from George. And I thought of
Andrew suggesting that Fran might return to Hollywood
with him, and if she'd done it, it would probably have
been the end of Paul. But the fact is, I don't think she'd
ever have considered going. She's quite as much in love
with Paul as he is with her, or more so, and I doubt if
anything would tear her away from him."

"So you don't think he murdered Andrew to prevent
her going away with him and cheating him out of her
fortune."

"I'm sure he didn't."

"And what about any other motive he might have had?"

"Can you think of one?"

"Not at the moment."

"Well, what about the other members of the family. Fran, Christine, George, the General?"

He had picked up one of the decayed chestnuts on the ground and was tossing it backwards and forwards from hand to hand, frowning at it as if it could tell him something.

"I don't know how often mothers and fathers murder their children," he said. "It's been known to happen, though more often when they're infants and not grown up and off their hands, and then not as often, I believe, as children have murdered their parents. A grandparent—well, I wouldn't say old man Searle was an impossibility if he knew, for instance, of something that Andrew intended to do that might injure Christine, or even Sonia. No, he isn't an impossibility, even if he's unlikely. And Fran . . ." He tossed the chestnut away and reached for a cigarette. "People blindly in love aren't always in an entirely rational state of mind, are they? If that's what she is with Paul, as you suggest, mightn't she imagine that Andrew was going to injure him somehow? He's in the accountancy department of Arne Webster, isn't he? Suppose he'd been fiddling things and Andrew had found it out."

"How could he do that, living in Hollywood and only arriving in England a day or so ago?"

"How indeed? Incidentally we don't know exactly when Andrew did arrive. All the same I don't find it a very convincing idea."

I stood up. "I think it's about time we were going in. It's nearly time for dinner. And I tell you what, Felix, I think whatever Christine says about wanting us to stay, I'm going home tomorrow. You can come with me if you want to."

He stood up too. "Sure about that?"

"Why not?"

"It's an invitation?"

"If that's how you like to take it."

"Then I'll probably come unless the police want us to stay here. Dawnay may prefer to keep us all together. But if he doesn't, I'd just as soon leave the Appleyards to themselves. I don't see what use we can be to them."

We started walking back towards the house.

We found the family gathered together over drinks in the drawing-room. But before joining them I decided to go upstairs to comb my hair, touch up my make-up, and try to do a little quiet thinking by myself. I wanted to go over the things about which Felix and I had been talking and find out if any of it meant anything to me. I was not really convinced by any of our arguments, and I was not sure that he had been either. Anyway, I wanted to be by myself for a little while, as I often do. I seem to need to be alone for a fair amount of time simply to remain myself. I turned towards the stairs, only to meet Ilse coming down them and to find that Felix was still at my elbow.

"Hello, Ilse," he said. "You look tired. I think you work too hard. It really can't be necessary in a household like this."

She did look tired, but she had plainly been up to her room, because she had changed out of her long, full-skirted dress into a tight black mini-skirt and a blouse of amazing brilliance, and substituted coral coloured plastic ear-rings for the green ones that she had been wearing earlier. Her tawny curls were loose on her shoulders.

She paused about three steps from the bottom of the staircase.

"I am not really tired," she said, "it is the emotion. I am accustomed to hard work, it never tires me, but not to emotion. I try to rest in my room for a little while after those policemen have gone, but I get so restless I cannot keep still and I change my dress to have something to do, which is ridiculous. Perhaps it is even improper at a time like this. I have a very grave dress of black with gold buttons, but no one in this house is wearing black, so I think if I do, though it suits me, perhaps it would look like a criticism."

"A very right and proper feeling," Felix said. "Tell me something, Ilse. Did you sleep well last night?"

"Oh yes, I always sleep very well. It is not because of that I am tired."

"You didn't wake up at all?"

I did not know what he was driving at.

"Oh yes, perhaps once, twice," she said. "I cannot remember."

"You don't remember if you heard anyone moving about downstairs at any time?"

So that was what he wanted to know.

"I think I remember I hear someone go to the bathroom," she said, "but I do not know when."

"Or who it was?"

"No. But I think it was General Searle. There are nights when the poor old gentleman cannot sleep, and he gets up and walks about the house and sometimes makes himself a drink, so perhaps that is really what I hear."

"But you aren't sure?"

"Oh no."

"Well, thank you, Ilse." Felix turned towards the drawing-room.

Ilse jumped down the remaining stairs in a single bound and I went up them to my room.

Dinner, as lunch had been, was a very silent meal, except that the General suddenly started to tell a story about something that had happened to a friend of his who had attempted an escape when he had been a prisoner of war in Germany during the Second World War. It was a long and pointless story, and I thought from the looks on their faces that everyone else there had heard it before, but silence was plainly something to which he was not accustomed and anything, however irrelevant, was to be preferred to it. It might conceal strange dangers if it was allowed to continue and even result in disastrous explosions.

After dinner I walked out on to the terrace and sat down in one of the chairs there, seeing the reflection of the moon in the still water of the swimming-pool, which no longer looked blue in that light, but was an oblong of darkness, just faintly touched with silver. Felix soon came and sat beside me and only a few minutes later Sonia joined us. She said nothing at first, though I had a feeling that she had come there with some purpose. But I was not at all prepared for what presently came.

In a cool, unemotional voice she suddenly remarked, "Of course you've realised, just as that detective has, that Andrew intended to murder David."

Ten _____

I WAS STARTLED. Felix, obviously, was not. He might
have been expecting Sonia to say just what she had when
she came to sit down with us. But he did not answer her.
He only looked her over thoughtfully and waited. She
began to get restive.

"Well, I'm sure you have, Felix, even if Virginia hasn't,"
she said.

"It's a possibility I had in mind, though I can't say I'm
absolutely convinced about it," he answered.

"What other explanation have you for that writing on
his lap?" she asked.

"I've no explanation at all."

"But there has to be one," she said.

"I don't quite accept that proposition," he said. "Some
things can remain entirely inexplicable, particularly in rela-
tion to human behaviour. And I'm not really quite sure
what your explanation is."

"Why, that Andrew was forging what he meant to look
like a suicide letter for David, whose body was going to be
found sooner or later somewhere or other."

"You couldn't say where or when?"

"Of course not. I don't know what he intended to do.
Perhaps it wasn't even serious."

"You mean he didn't really intend to murder David? He was just having fun with the idea and didn't realise he'd already been murdered himself."

' "I suppose in a way that's what I really mean," she said. "After all, he couldn't have got at David last night, could he? And today David and I were going to Crete. We were going to spend a fortnight there. And if you think it was absurd for us to have a honeymoon, the fact is it was just a couple of weeks' holiday that David had due to him, and I'd managed to arrange to have the same time off myself, and it wasn't a real honeymoon at all. Actually I can't imagine ever wanting a honeymoon, though I suppose once upon a time it was the time when you lost your virginity without friends and neighbours being able to watch the way it turned out."

"And what were you going to do when you got home?" Felix asked.

"Go back to work. Go back to our flat."

"In Fulham, isn't it?"

"Yes, you know that perfectly well. You've been there."

He nodded. He was smoking one of his eternal cigarettes and drew on it now and breathed smoke out before going on. He was no longer looking at Sonia, but at the dark pool with its sheen of silver.

"So," he said, "you think that what happened last night was only a sort of rehearsal."

"That's how I see it," she said with an increase of eagerness. "I think he'd decided to try to murder David some time. I don't know when he thought of it. I don't know if it's really why he came here yesterday, but then he realised that with David staying at The Barley Mow he'd have no chance of doing it right away. All the same, when he was sitting in his room alone and perhaps couldn't sleep, he went ahead with his plan and drafted a letter that was to be left by David's body sometime, I suppose in our flat in London. And that draft is the letter they found in his room which they say is genuinely in Andrew's writing. I don't know if you noticed something a little odd in the wording of that letter. He said he saw it in my eyes that evening that I didn't love him. *That* evening. Which sounds as if it might have been referring to some evening some time ago, not just to last night, doesn't it?"

Felix nodded. "Yes, I noticed it," he said.

"And then Andrew settled down to copy that letter in David's writing. I know they've written to each other several times since Andrew went away, so he'd have had some letter of David's to work from and may have been practicing it for a long time. And perhaps what began as a kind of pretence, almost a sort of game, gradually took hold of him, and perhaps hearing that David and I were actually going to get married triggered off some craziness in Andrew's brain. As a matter of fact . . ." She paused and drew a long breath. "As a matter of fact, there was always something in Andrew I was a little afraid of. That was partly the reason I ran away from him when we were on the edge of getting married. When I told Christine that it was because I was against the marriage of first cousins and that I thought that was one reason our child, if he'd been born alive, would have been abnormal, that was only part of the truth. It was the way Andrew took my wanting to break our engagement that really made me run away from him. He was . . . Oh, I can't describe it, but he frightened me."

"So now let me make sure I understand what you've been saying," Felix said. "You think Andrew had always been in love with you and long ago, enough for him to have had time to practice copying David's writing, he'd thought of murdering him. And he'd decided that however he finally did it, it was to look like suicide. And last night he sat down and to pass the time drafted a letter which he meant to copy and on some occasion leave by David's body. And presently he started copying this letter in his best effort at forging David's writing. But between his making the draft and starting to copy it he'd had a drink with someone who came into the bungalow to visit him, and the drink he'd had was heavily laced with Somnolin or some other drug, and almost as soon as he started to make the copy he collapsed and passed out and died. Of course you realise what you're doing, don't you?"

She looked puzzled. "What I'm doing?"

"You're putting a noose round David's neck. You're providing him with the best of motives for Andrew's murder."

Her face went blank, as if this really had not occurred to her. "A noose?"

"Never mind, that's only figurative," Felix said consolingly. "We don't actually hang people any more in this country. The old phrase just slipped out."

"But how could he have had a motive for killing Andrew?" she asked. "He didn't know what was in Andrew's mind."

"No, I suppose that's probably true."

"Of course he didn't. He hadn't any conceivable motive." But her voice was tremulous. "He really hadn't."

"So we're back to the troublesome question of who had," Felix said. "Virginia and I were talking that over before dinner and we got nowhere."

She stood up abruptly.

"I wish I hadn't talked to you," she said. "You're only twisting what I tried to say. I think the evidence that Andrew was thinking of killing David is very strong, but it doesn't have to mean that David was thinking of killing Andrew."

She swept in through the french window behind us.

"And of course she's perfectly right," Felix said. "There's no logical connection between the two things. All the same . . ."

"Well?" I said when he paused.

"Nothing," he said. "I wish we could think about something else for a little while."

"Such as?"

"Oh, anything. You and me perhaps, though that's a hackneyed old subject. No, what about the state of the economy, or who's going to win the next election when it happens, or the greenhouse effect, or the environment. Something it's really safe to talk about without getting excited."

"I'm sure there are lots of people who can get excited about all those things," I said.

"Do you really?"

"Yes, of course, or one wouldn't hear so much about them on television. Without them people simply wouldn't turn on the news."

"But murder's still the champion for arousing interest, even on television."

"I thought you didn't want to talk about it."

"I don't."

"Then let's go inside. No one there will be talking about it, or even anything else much. There'll be what I think is sometimes called a conspiracy of silence. Then we'll all go to bed and no one will get any sleep to speak of."

"All right, let's go in." He stood up. "Virginia, I'd love you so much if you'd only let me."

"I can't think why," I said. "I'm always horrid to you."

"And talking about it doesn't excite you any more than talking about the environment."

"I can get quite excited about the environment when I try," I said. "Just stay quite still for a moment and listen. Can't you hear the traffic on that motorway? It's true there isn't much at this time of the evening, but when I grew up in Allingford there were only meadows there and an old horse track and a pretty lane. Sitting out here one might even have heard a nightingale."

"What about the odd German bomb from time to time? You were the right age for those, weren't you?"

"Yes, there was that, of course. Nothing's perfect."

He gave me a hand to haul me out of my chair.

"Come along. Let's go in."

We went into the drawing-room.

But I was wrong that there would be no further talk of murder. As we entered the room David and Paul were just leaving to return to The Barley Mow, George and Fran had settled down to a game of chess, Christine was slumped in a chair and in an attitude of complete exhaustion looked asleep, and General Searle was standing with his back to the empty fireplace, talking to no one in particular. That is to say, no one in particular seemed to be listening to him, though his voice was emphatic and somewhat hoarse, as if he had already been talking for some time.

"That's who it has to be," he said. "In my view there's no question of it. Dig a little and you'll find them all, means, motive, and opportunity. Someone like her almost certainly had access to drugs. Probably is on them herself. Motive—well, none of us think Andrew was an angel. I'd guess he had an affair with her and was trying to break it off. That's why he came here. He wanted to let her understand the kind of background he came from and that she didn't belong in it. Opportunity—if she arrived at the bungalow late in the evening and wanted to talk to him, he wouldn't actually have turned her away, would he? He'd have let her in and had a drink with her. . . . George, are you listening?"

George moved a knight and took a bishop of Fran's.

"There, you see, you shouldn't have moved that pawn," he said. "It was covering the bishop till you did that."

"And now I can take your knight," she said. She moved her queen swiftly from somewhere far away on the board and snatched his knight off it.

"Um—yes—well, I see, that's what you were counting on," George said.

The General turned to Felix and me.

"They haven't been listening to me," he said.

"You were talking about that woman in pink, I presume," Felix answered.

"Ah, you understand that, do you? Good, good."

"Only I'm not sure if you've explained the forgeries," Felix said. "Is she responsible for them too?"

"For the one that claimed that Andrew was dying of an incurable disease, of course." The General shook a finger in the air as if he were giving a lecture to some not very tractable pupils. "Doesn't that woman seem more likely than anyone else we know of? If she'd been in America with Andrew, she may have known of his fall and thought that if any questions were asked the probability that he'd banged his head then would account for everything."

"You know, I thought that letter was rather well written," Felix said. "Even rather moving. When I first read it I didn't doubt for a moment that it was genuine. And the forgery appears to have been a clever one. Could the kind of person that that woman was really have done a job like that?"

"Got it done for her by some connection of hers," the General said. "People like that probably have connections with all kinds in the criminal fraternity. It might have been some artist she knew who could turn his hand to a bit of forgery when funds ran out. I don't suppose for a moment she wrote it herself. But the man who did it for her may even have come down to Allingford with her and be in the same hotel or boarding house there now, the two of them having waited till they got here to make their plans about how they were to get at Andrew. And he must have known where she was going to stay, whether or not she had her forger friend with her, and have let her know that he'd be in the bungalow. That was just perfect for her, of course."

"Check!" Fran said.

"My God, yes, I ought to have seen that coming," George replied. "Not mate, however. There, I think I've got out of that spot of trouble now."

"If the police can find that woman, it'll be check mate for her," General Searle said. "You said she arrived in a white Mini, didn't you, Felix?"

"Yes," Felix said.

"So if Andrew came down in it with her, inquiries at the station won't tell them anything. But I suppose the police can check when he arrived from America and whether or not he was travelling alone. Was it your impression she might be American?"

"She didn't say a word when we saw her," Felix said. "She just bolted from the room. As far as accent goes, she could have been anything. That is . . ." He paused abruptly and I wondered what had just occurred to him.

But the General did not seem to notice the pause. He went on, "Of course the police will find her sooner or later. Wonderful what they can do nowadays. Wonderful people. Sometimes I used to wish I'd gone into the police instead of the army, but I dare say I'm not clever enough. Christine!"

She sat up with a jerk. "Yes, Father?"

"I'm going to bed. I'm very tired. That's what you ought to do too. You're quite worn out."

She stood up, stretched, and yawned.

"Yes, I think I'll do that. Felix, do you mind staying in that bungalow after—after what's happened. There's a little room upstairs you could have if you'd prefer it."

"No, thank you, Christine, I'll be all right there," he answered.

But I had a feeling that he would not leave his french window open that night, even though there seemed to be no rational reason for a poisoner to return, unless just possibly to make sure that Felix had not seen him the night before. But it seemed to me that he would probably feel that to keep out of the way would be altogether wiser.

My own night was quiet enough, but I did not sleep much. Only towards morning I fell into a truly deep sleep from which I was wakened by Ilse, bringing me tea. Presently I went downstairs and found Christine sitting alone at the breakfast table. She was in her jeans and a man's shirt again. I thought from the look of her face that she had slept even less than I had. She poured out coffee for me and pushed corn flakes towards me, but did not greet me.

After a minute or two I said, "Christine, wouldn't it be best for Felix and me to go home this morning?"

She gave a listless shrug of her shoulders.

"If you want to, of course, Virginia," she answered.

"Can we help by staying?"

"I don't see how anybody can help."

"Then suppose we do go."

"Yes, if you want to," she repeated wearily. "The police will know where to find you if they want you."

"You haven't heard anything more from them yet?"

"No, but Dr. Burrows phoned just a little while ago and said he was coming out to see us. It seems he's got something to tell us."

"About the post mortem?"

"I suppose so." She put both elbows on the table and took her head in her hands. "Oh God, Virginia, I was so happy when Andrew walked in, and now I'd give anything if he'd stayed in America for ever. Sonia and David would have had their wedding yesterday and by today they'd be in Crete already, and I'd have been feeling dog tired and complaining about the unnecessary fuss and clearing up there was to do, and worrying about packing up the presents, and feeling so happy. There's something rather marvellous about feeling very tired when you've really been enjoying yourself. But I'm sorry you've had such a miserable visit."

I did not trouble to say that that was a minor part of what had befallen, because of course she knew it. Soon Felix came in, then Fran and eventually George. General Searle was last. Sonia, it appeared, did not want any breakfast.

It was about half-past nine when Dr. Burrows appeared. He came into the room with his usual look of thrusting energy, but then seemed reluctant to talk. He accepted coffee, sat down, coughed, and said in his soft voice, which could sound so intimate, "Well, of course I don't know what it means, but I felt I'd better come. I'm not sure that the police will think I should, but after all we're friends, or I like to think so, and—well, I decided to come anyway."

"For God's sake, man, what have you got to tell us?" George demanded, his bulging eyes looking fierce.

"Not very much actually," the young doctor said. "And perhaps it's premature, because the important guy hasn't really finished his job. But it appears that your son had a lot of alcohol and a good deal of a drug, probably Somnolin, in his system, and there are signs that he'd broken a rib recently, but otherwise he appears to have been in perfect health. They've found no signs yet that he was suffering from some serious, lingering disease."

"What about his head?" Fran broke in.

"His head?" Dr. Burrows looked puzzled.

"Yes, when he fell couldn't he have hit his head and perhaps damaged his brain?" she asked.

"I haven't been told anything of the kind," Dr. Burrows said.

"I think that's what happened," she said. "He seemed quite normal when he got here, but really he wasn't sane. That's why he wrote the letter saying he was killing himself because Sonia didn't love him, and really it was why he killed himself too."

"Aren't you forgetting the forged letter, which said he'd a mortal illness?" George said.

"Oh no, I know who wrote that," she answered.

He looked extremely startled and prepared to become angry with her. "You don't know anything, Fran. Keep quiet for once, can't you?"

"But don't you see, it wasn't a forgery, he wrote it himself," she said. "People's handwriting can change completely when they want it to, don't you know that? Look how mine's changed in the last year or two. Compare the way I write now with the way I wrote when I was at school. You'd never dream it was the same person writing. And he made up that story about his being so ill just to spare Sonia. In the state of mind he was in he'd have forgotten that a post mortem would get at the truth, and he wrote that carefully prepared letter in his new, very neat writing, then he took the drug and as it began to work he forgot he'd written it and wrote a second letter in his old writing and even began to write another in David's, because he wanted so much to be David. I explained that to you before."

"Never heard such a load of rubbish in my life!" General Searle exploded. "The man was murdered."

Sonia walked in.

"Good morning, Dr. Burrows," she said quietly. "I suppose you came to tell them all that I've been on Somnolin for a couple of years and that you gave me a new prescription for some only a few days ago."

Eleven

DR. BURROWS drew himself up to his full, not very great height.

"I have said nothing about it," he said with dignity. "That was a purely professional matter."

"Then why did you come?"

Christine exclaimed impatiently, "Oh, Sonia, why do you always try to make yourself the centre of everything? One wouldn't think it of you, you seem so quiet, but I've noticed before it's what you always do. It's why you wanted the wedding. Dr. Burrows came here to give us some very interesting information."

"All the same, it's true, I'd a bottle of Somnolin from him only a few days ago, and now it's empty," Sonia said. "If you look in my room, you'll find it."

"How does it come to have emptied itself in a few days?" George asked truculently.

"Can't you guess? I gave them all to Andrew in a drink last night," she said.

"Don't be absurd," he said. "That isn't funny."

"I didn't mean it to be. It's simply what the police will get around to thinking, isn't it?"

"If you try to make them believe it, perhaps they will. What really happened to the pills?"

"I flushed them down the lavatory."

"In Heaven's name, why?"

"Because I'm a fool."

"I don't propose to argue about that," he said, "but I'd like a proper answer to my question too."

She dropped into a chair at the table. "All right, I did it because I was frightened. I thought, 'I'm becoming an addict. Here I am, getting married tomorrow and I can't face it without taking pills tonight. If this marriage means anything it ought to be the beginning of a new life. Start facing things without taking pills.' So I flushed the lot down the drain."

"But you've never taken many," Dr. Burrows said, looking worried, "unless you've been getting them from someone else besides me. I can't say offhand how long ago I prescribed the last lot for you, but it's at least several months. The occasional pill couldn't possibly have done you any harm."

"I take them sometimes myself," Christine said. "I took one on Friday night. I'd got into such an excited state, what with Andrew arriving and all, and I was afraid of not being able to cope with things next day, so I took one and had a good night's sleep, that's all that happened."

"All the same, I thought it was time I stopped," Sonia said. "I didn't like the feeling that I was getting dependent on them. I'd got into the habit of taking them every time anything interesting or exciting was going to happen next day because of a feeling like the one you had, Christine, that perhaps I shouldn't be able to cope if I didn't. And now, of course, I'm wishing to God I hadn't been such a fool as to ditch the lot, because last night I really needed one. And now there's the empty bottle there and Dr. Burrows to say he prescribed a hundred for me only a few days ago, and none of you really believe what I've told you."

"Who says we don't?" George demanded.

"I can see it on your faces."

"Nonsense," the General said. "Why has everyone suddenly taken to talking nonsense? If we look as if we don't believe you, it's because we didn't believe you were such a fool as you seem to be. Christine's quite right, you like to see yourself in the centre of everything. Never noticed it myself till now, but it's perfectly correct. You know, if that letter written by poor Andrew saying he was killing himself for love of you wasn't genuine, instead of the other one, I'd be inclined to think it was you who forged it."

"Father, there's no need to be quite so horrid," Christine said. "That letter *was* genuine."

"I wonder, I wonder," the General muttered. "A peculiar letter, a hell of a lot of dope missing, a bloody hysterical woman. . . . No, no, Sonia, I'm sorry, of course we believe you. I don't want to be unkind. Whether or not the police will believe you is of course another matter. I presume you mean to tell them what you've told us."

"Of course," she said. "Meanwhile, suppose you tell me why Dr. Burrows really came, if it was nothing to do with my pills."

"Simply to tell us that as far as they've been able to discover at the moment," George said, "Andrew had a large quantity of alcohol and some drug in his stomach, and that otherwise he appeared to be in perfect health. The forged letter in which he was supposed to have said that he was suffering from some incurable illness was quite off the mark. Why anyone should have made a blunder like that I don't know."

"I suppose it's possible, if your son's real letter hadn't been found," Dr. Burrows said, "that there wouldn't have been a post mortem. I might have signed the death certificate myself. It was only that second letter turning up that made his death look suspicious. And the letter a suicide leaves behind isn't usually forged. Again, but for the second letter, it might never have been examined by an expert."

There were voices outside in the hall and David and Paul came into the room.

Like everyone else there, except for the doctor, they both had the slightly bleached look of people who have not slept well.

"But if we're in the way, we'll push off," David said. "We've kept our rooms on at The Barley Mow in case you wanted us to stay on."

"Of course you must stay," Christine answered. "For Sonia's sake, for all of us, please stay."

David went to Sonia and kissed her on the forehead.

"Not quite what we planned, is it?" he said.

She caught at his hand and clung to it fiercely.

"But we'll still go to Crete," she said. "If not today, then tomorrow or the day after that or some time. We aren't going to let our lives be ruined by what's happened."

"No," he said, but sounded as if he were not quite sure of this. "Of course not. Good morning, Dr. Burrows. What's brought you?"

He and Paul then had to be told what had brought the doctor. They both accepted it without comment, and Dr. Burrows said that he had better be leaving, but that of course if there was any way in which he could help, he should be called.

As soon as he had gone, Fran announced, "I'm going to swim. I just can't stand this sitting around, talking and talking. Nobody listens to what I've got to say, though I'm the only one who's explained anything, so I'm going to swim. Paul, why don't you come in with me?"

He did not look enthusiastic, but said uncertainly, "If General Searle will lend me his swimming trunks again . . ."

"Of course, of course," the General said. "Fran's right for once, it'll do you good."

She and Paul both left the room and only a few minutes later were back again in their swimming gear and went out to the pool, which again in the sunshine was a glittering blue. The General asked if no one else felt like joining them, but heads were shaken, though Sonia and David went out together and sat down on the terrace. It was only as that happened that I noticed that Felix was not in the room.

I did not think much about it and even when he returned I did not think of asking him where he had been, though it did occur to me as slightly odd that he had apparently been upstairs and not to his room in the bungalow. Martha came in then and started to clear the breakfast away, and Christine went out to the kitchen with her, no doubt to discuss arrangements for the day with Mrs. Grantly. The General picked up the Sunday newspaper and wandered away with it to the library. George scowled when he could not find the paper, then strode out into the garden, and I saw him setting off for what looked like a brisk walk into the park.

Finding myself alone with Felix, I did ask him at last, "What took you prowling around upstairs?"

"Just looking into a few things," he said. "With all of them down here it seemed a good time to do it. Pity I've no chance to do it at The Barley Mow. What Sonia says appears to have been true."

"About those pills she had?"

"Yes. There's an empty bottle in her room with her name on it, and Dr. Burrows', and the name of the stuff,

Somnolin, with the dosage one or two at night. But you know, the bottle in Andrew's room didn't have Dr. Burrows' name on it, or anything about a dosage. It just had a label saying Somnolin. It could have come, as the letter said, direct from the Arne Webster, not from any doctor. Then, while I was at it, I thought I'd look in the other bedrooms and there's a bottle of the stuff in George and Christine's room, but it's nearly full, and there's no sign of anything of the sort in the General's room, or in Fran's, or in the bathrooms."

"But didn't Ilse tell us that the General sometimes doesn't sleep well and goes wandering about the house?" I said.

"Yes, that's his remedy for insomnia, not pills," Felix said. "He walks around and gets himself a drink."

"Then do you think it's possible . . . ?" I paused.

"That he saw something that evening?" Felix said, reading my mind as he often did too easily. "And is keeping quiet about it because it's to do with the family. But he wouldn't have seen anyone go into the bungalow, if it was by the french window they went in. The windows there face away from the house. If someone came up to Andrew's room across the lawn at the back, it wouldn't have been visible from the house. And nor would a light if Andrew had kept his on, which I suppose he did, anyway while his visitor was with him, having that last drink."

"Felix, was Andrew's light on when you went into his room in the morning?" I asked.

"No, as a matter of fact, it wasn't. And it would have been, wouldn't it, if he'd been writing that curious scrap of a letter or whatever it was that was on his lap when he passed out? He wouldn't have tried to do any writing in the dark, even if he was half-dead already from the drug he'd taken. So my theory that his visitor came back to leave the forged letter really looks like being correct."

"You don't think Ilse turned the light out when she went into the room in the morning?"

"No, as a matter of fact, I asked her that, and she's sure she didn't."

"So you've thought of all this already."

"And so have the police, you can take it from me."

"I wonder—do you think it's possible that two people did the job? One to give Andrew the drug in the drink and one to go in later to leave the letter?"

"It isn't impossible," Felix said. "Of course, you're thinking of David and Sonia."

"I wasn't thinking of anyone in particular. There's always that woman in pink."

"That oh, so convenient woman in pink!"

"Well, she's real, isn't she, even if she hasn't been explained? We both saw her. She's not a delusion."

"And so did Bob and Ilse. All the same, suppose it turned out that it's a case of what you could call communal delusion. I'm sure I've heard of that happening. 'There are more things in heaven and earth . . .' All right, all right, I won't go on. But I've had one or two very strange experiences myself. Have I told you about the time I was sitting in a friend's room and the door opened and a man dressed in the uniform of the First World War came in and walked to the window and opened it and threw himself out? And my friend said, 'You saw him, didn't you?' And I said I had and she said, 'Thank God, I've been afraid I was going mad. He comes here always on the first of the month. Poor man, he was badly shell-shocked and he came home on leave and threw himself out of the window sooner than go back to the front, and now he can't stop doing it. I usually try to be away on the first of the month, I feel so sorry for him.' "

"And did you find the window open or closed when he'd thrown himself out?" I asked.

"Oh, closed. Of course he hadn't been there at all. But we'd both seen him."

"Felix, I wish you'd stick to detecting instead of to having strange experiences, it suits you better," I said. "Besides, I think I read that story in a magazine somewhere. And as for our woman who stole Sonia's necklace, do you think that mere delusions steal necklaces?"

The door was flung open. Ilse came bounding in.

"Please!" she cried. "Please, where is everyone? It is most urgent."

We both stood up.

"Is it the police?" Felix asked.

"No, no, no police, it is Bob," she answered.

"Bob? Has he hurt himself?"

"No, but he has been telling. He tells me things and I tell him he must tell everyone, but he says it isn't his business. But it is his business, it is very much his business, but he says he doesn't like to get mixed up in things. So I say, 'No one likes to get mixed up in things, but one has a duty to do.' So he says, 'All right, you go and talk.' But that is not the same thing, we must find everyone, or at least Mr. and Mrs. Appleyard, and Bob will talk to them."

In the end we managed to collect Christine and the General and Sonia and David and even George, who returned when David pursued him into the park and told him that something seemed to have come up that made his presence necessary.

But Fran and Paul stayed sitting on the edge of the pool with their feet dangling in the water and looking as if they were deep in a very engrossing conversation. They paid no attention when Christine called out to them that they should join us in the drawing-room. I wondered if Fran had got around to asking Paul to marry her. It looked rather like it.

Meanwhile, Ilse had produced Bob, who looked embarrassed and a little stubborn, as if he did not like having her dictate to him.

When Christine asked him what had happened, he cleared his throat and said, "Well." There he paused.

"Well, what?" George asked.

"It probably isn't anything," Bob said.

"Never mind if it isn't," George said. "What's worrying you?"

"It's just a talk I had with a bloke I know," Bob said. "I mean, we were both in the pub, The Barley Mow, yesterday evening, and we got talking. I'd gone down there for a drink last thing, I mean, and he was there and we talked about all the things that have been happening here, and he said, 'You're talking about Jon Sanchez, the actor, are you? Saw him in a film last Saturday.'"

"Who was this bloke?" George asked.

"Ern Whistler, drives a taxi," Bob replied.

"And what did he have to say, apart from having seen one of my son's films?"

"Drove him from the station Friday evening. Drove him here. That's all."

"Wait a minute, wait a minute!" George exclaimed. "This may be important, Bob. Your friend picked my son up at the station and drove him straight here?"

"I wouldn't say Ern's a friend of mine," Bob said. "I mean, he's just someone I know."

"All right, but you think he'd be telling the truth?"

"Likely he would about a thing like that."

"But not about other things?"

"Oh yes, never caught him out in anything myself," Bob answered, anxious not to commit himself.

"But listen, Bob, your friend, that is, your acquaintance, picked my son up at the station in Allingford on Friday evening and drove him here?"

"That's right."

"At the station, not somewhere in the town?"

"That's what he said."

"Did he say what train it was he'd met?"

"The six-five, getting here when he did, it must've been."

"Yes," George nodded. "The six-five." He turned to Christine. "And that means he wasn't at Arne Webster in the afternoon. And you see what that means."

"That that letter about his illness was altogether false," she answered. "Of course he could have got some Somnolin somewhere else, but he didn't get it at the Arne Webster.

"Furthermore," General Searle said, "it means that something I've been inclined to believe is quite mistaken. Andrew didn't drive down to Allingford with that woman in her white Mini and just pick up a taxi in the town so as not to be seen arriving here with her. He must have been in contact with her sometime after arriving from America, but he didn't drive down here with her."

George looked at Bob.

"I suppose your friend didn't say anything about seeing a white Mini at The Barley Mow or anywhere else any time on Friday or Saturday?"

Bob shook his head. "Didn't think of asking him."

"No, of course not. Well, thank you, Bob. What you've told us is very interesting."

"My pleasure," Bob said, and left us.

I think it was only after he had gone that I realised that

all of us in the room were looking rather curiously at David, and that he, in a quiet way, was furiously angry. Angry or afraid, it is sometimes difficult to tell the difference between the two states. For of everyone in the household there was no question that he was the person who could most easily have helped himself to some Somnolin at Arne Webster without arousing any notice from anyone.

Not that the fact that Andrew could not have been at the Institute in the afternoon, as the forged letter said, meant very much, since we already knew that that letter was a lie from beginning to end. Yet perhaps we had all of us had some lingering thought that there might be some truth in it, even if it had not been written by Andrew himself, almost as if we felt that he might have written what was in it, if he had still been alive to do it. Then suddenly I began to wonder if Sonia actually believed that David had acquired the Somnolin.

Was that the real reason why she had flushed her own Somnolin down the lavatory, not a day or two ago, as she had said, but this morning? Had she deliberately done something suspicious to draw suspicion away from him to herself? If so, she had acted her part very well, but then there was a trace of acting ability in all this family, and I knew that there were depths in her of which I had little understanding.

It was about half an hour later that the police arrived once more. It was Superintendent Dawnay and Sergeant Wells again, and they both had singularly expressionless faces of the kind that tell you far more than if they had had frowns or smiles or any sort of animation. It was obvious that they had something very unpleasant to impart.

Addressing George, the Superintendent said, "We've found the woman, sir."

"The woman?" George said. "The woman in pink?"

"Yes, she's wearing pink," the Superintendent answered, "though it's somewhat stained with blood. Very nasty. Stab wound in the neck. She was found in her car this morning in Reservoir Lane."

"Dead!" the General exclaimed. "And in Reservoir Lane —that's quite near here!"

"That's right, sir," the detective said. "Just a lead off after that motorway junction."

Twelve

I REMEMBER Reservoir Lane as only a little way from the end of what was left of Oldenham Park, which once had spread far beyond its present precincts, though bit by bit it had been sold off by the family who had owned it before George's father had bought it from them. Even he, though his income had not been shrinking, had sold a certain amount of it to a neighbouring farmer in order to make it a more convenient unit to maintain. From the lane to the village across the park could not have been more than a mile and a half, if as much.

We were all staring at the Superintendent and none of us, after the General, appeared to have anything to say. I wondered if I ought to call Fran and Paul into the room, as this was a matter of such great importance to all the family, but before I could do so George pulled himself together.

"Do you know who she is?" he asked.

"A Mrs. Margaret Macinnes," the Superintendent answered. "She had a driving licence and a banker's card and a cheque-book in her handbag, which appear to identify her fairly positively."

"Do you know where she lived?" George asked.

"In a flat, No. 2A Beverley Gardens, Islington."

"And have you checked that?"

"We've checked that a Mrs. Margaret Macinnes lived at that address for the last two years. She was a widow. Her husband was killed in a car crash about three months ago."

"Not also by a stab wound in the neck!"

"No, to the best of our knowledge, he was driving over the legal limit, hit a tree, was thrown through the windscreen, and died on the spot. So far as we know, there was nothing suspicious about his death."

It is hard for me to say just when it happened, but sometime during this exchange I became sure that the name Margaret Macinnes meant something to Felix. There was no obvious change in his face to make me think this, yet I knew it so well that even a slight flicker of his eyelids could convey something to me. I remembered besides that he had said to me that he had a kind of feeling that he had seen the woman before. But he did not appear to be in a mood to volunteer anything to the police.

Superintendent Dawnay was continuing. "She was found in her car about eight o'clock this morning by a man who was cycling past. He lives in one of those cottages at the far end of the lane and was on his way to the garage in Oldenham that stays open on Sundays to pick up his usual Sunday paper. He saw a car pulled off the road by a gate into one of the fields there, and he was about simply to ride on when it struck him that the car was parked at rather an odd angle and he thought that perhaps he should make sure that there was nothing wrong. And he found the woman inside, fallen forward over the steering wheel, with gashes in her neck and dried blood all over her and the inside of the car. He rode on into Oldenham and phoned us, then rode back to the car and waited for us. His statement appears to be completely straightforward."

"Dried blood!" David exclaimed. "Then she'd been dead for some time."

"So it would appear," the Superintendent said.

"Do you know how long?" David asked.

"The doctor's guess at the moment is that she was killed around midnight, though naturally that's only a rough estimate."

"Is that Dr. Burrows?"

"No, it's our own man in Allingford."

"And you're sure it was the same woman who was seen here yesterday by Mr. and Mrs. Freer?"

"No, of course we're not sure until they've identified her. But she was wearing a pink silk suit and had blonde hair, and there were some broken spectacles on the floor of the car and the number of the car she was in was the number given to us by Mr. Freer yesterday." He turned to Felix with a slight narrowing of the pale eyes in his brown face. "And she had what I believe is your telephone number in a notebook she carried, sir." He recited a number and I knew it was Felix's. "Is that yours?"

Felix nodded dubiously, as if he found it difficult to remember his own number.

"Yes," he said, "it's mine. And you said her name was Macinnes."

"Yes, does that mean anything to you?"

"Not a thing. Very puzzling. It doesn't mean anything at all to me. But you've checked that it's really her name, have you?"

"Only that a woman called Margaret Macinnes has been living at 2A Beverley Gardens, Islington, for the last two years, that her husband, Arthur Macinnes, was killed recently in a car crash and that she had a Mini with the number you gave us. Also, that she isn't at her home now. But it's still conceivable that she isn't the woman you saw here yesterday, though I should be surprised if it turns out that she isn't. I'm afraid I must ask you and your wife to come to the mortuary to identify her. I'm sorry about it, but it's of some importance."

Felix looked round the room.

"Does the name Margaret Macinnes mean anything to any of you here?"

Nobody answered.

I wished that I could be alone with Felix to ask him what the name meant to him, because I was certain that it meant something. But for me to say so at the moment, apart from putting him in an uncomfortable position, which is something I am always inclined to try to avoid doing even when there is a good deal of provocation, would not achieve anything, as I had nothing much more than an intuition to go on. I thought that I would leave it to the police to inquire what his telephone number was doing in the woman's notebook.

"Funny thing," General Searle observed, "I remember reading about an Arthur Macinnes being killed in a car crash. I used to know an Arthur Macinnes slightly some years ago and I wondered if it was him. It sounded quite likely. Poor old Macinnes, I thought always did drink too much—menace on the road—shouldn't be allowed. But the police can't be everywhere, can they? I sympathise with you chaps. If there's say a plane crash and a few dozen people are killed, it's on television night after night and there are funds got up for the grieving relatives, but you can slaughter thousands on the roads and no one seems to worry about it except the people who happened to know them and who hardly get a dime. Seems out of proportion somehow. However, this Mrs. Macinnes wasn't killed in a car crash, that was her husband. She was murdered. Different matter entirely."

"What about the weapon?" George asked. "Have you got it?"

"Yes, it was left in the car, but there are no fingerprints on it," the Superintendent answered. "One could hardly hope for that."

"But what was it?"

"A common or garden kitchen knife, brand new by the look of it. Might have been bought for the purpose."

I heard Felix give a small exclamation, then he went quickly out of the room.

"And it could have been done by a man or a woman," George said. "Is that right?"

"I should say so, yes," the Superintendent agreed.

"Would he or she have got blood on themselves?"

"Possibly, but not necessarily. Presumably whoever it was, was sitting beside Mrs. Macinnes in the passenger seat, and when the attack was made knew that there'd be a spurt of blood and so was careful to protect himself from it."

"Had the car stopped by then?"

"We think so, or it wouldn't simply have turned into that gateway, it would have crashed into the ditch."

"But you said it was parked at an odd angle."

"Yes, I imagine Mrs. Macinnes was already being threatened and was told to swing off the road at that point, or her murderer may even have grabbed the wheel and made her turn there. Of course an examination is proceeding for finger-prints in the car and foot-prints and for traces of blood near it, but nothing has been found so far. It's early to give an opinion, however."

Felix returned to the room.

"It may be of a good deal of interest to you, Superintendent," he said, "that a large kitchen knife that appears to have been given to Miss Capel as a wedding present is missing now. I remember noticing it on Friday. It was part of a set of knives on the sort of bracket that's meant to be put up on the wall. There were three altogether, but the biggest one is gone."

"Show me!" the Superintendent said.

Felix went out of the room again, this time followed by the two detectives.

Christine looked at Sonia and said, "That's the present Mrs. Grantly gave you. I thought it such a good idea, compared with the china shepherdess or something like that which I was afraid she'd probably give you. So embarrassing to know what to do with things like that, short of accidentally dropping them."

Sonia nodded apprehensively. "Of course you see what it means, don't you?"

"That someone, one of us, or someone who somehow got into the house yesterday, must have been the murderer," Christine answered, her soft voice as shrill as I had ever heard it. "That can't be true. It isn't true. There's got to be some other explanation."

"I can think of one," I said, deciding for once to take an active part in what was happening. "Suppose that woman, Mrs. Macinnes, stole the knife at the same time as the necklace, and suppose she picked someone up in her car and they had a quarrel, perhaps about the necklace, and after turning off the lane she threatened him with the knife and there was a struggle and he got it away from her and killed her. The Superintendent hasn't said anything about the necklace so far."

"So the motive for her murder might have been robbery and nothing to do with us." George looked intensely grateful to me. "That's a very interesting idea, Virginia."

"It's only a suggestion," I said, not really feeling very convinced by it myself. But they had all looked so appalled at the thought that it might be one of themselves who had taken the knife that I had felt that I had to contribute something.

After a minute or two Felix returned once more, followed by the other two men.

"The missing knife was part of a set that matches the one we found in the car," the Superintendent said. "Of course that doesn't make it certain that it came from here, but it looks probable."

"Go on, George, tell Mr. Dawnay Virginia's idea," Christine said. "I think it's much more likely to be right than that any of us here murdered that woman."

George obediently repeated what I had said.

The Superintendent nodded as if he was prepared to give my suggestion some consideration, since almost anything, when it came to murder, might be credible, but he did not look deeply interested in it. Nor was I myself. Only when I looked round the room I found it almost impossible to imagine that anyone there would be capable of a violent killing. Murder by the overdose of a drug, the forging of a letter, these did not seem quite so improbable, but violence seemed out of character. But just then Fran and Paul came into the room and I suddenly found myself wondering if Paul could be violent.

I could imagine that he might be, given the provocation, and I supposed that General Searle, at some time during his career in the Army, might have done some killing, or at least faced up the danger of being killed himself, and that a capacity for violence might not be buried so very deeply under his kindly, elderly personality. But what would he have been doing, driving along Reservoir Lane, which led nowhere, with the woman in pink?

Fran and Paul were hand in hand and Fran's face was

radiant. Paul's had a trace of embarrassment on it, nevertheless he seemed to find it difficult not to smile.

"Paul and I have something wonderful to tell you," Fran said excitedly. "We decided to tell you at once—"

"Keep it to yourselves!" Sonia exploded. "We can see what it is and this isn't the best time to talk about it. You'd better listen to what we've got to tell you. Superintendent, will you please tell them what you've told us?"

"But this'll only take a minute," Fran began, when Sonia broke in again, "Be quiet and listen!"

The Superintendent repeated quickly what he had told the rest of us, and as he spoke the radiance faded from Fran's face and the embarrassment from Paul's, where it was replaced by a look of puzzled intentness. When my suggestion was expounded to him he gave me a long, thoughtful look, as if he were wondering how serious I had been.

"And the necklace?" he said. "No one's said anything about the necklace. Is it missing?"

The Superintendent did not reply, though I had an uneasy feeling that he might have been able to do so if he had thought it advisable. But no one else seemed to share my feeling.

"If it is, Mrs. Freer just might be right and the motive for the woman's murder have been robbery," Paul said.

"On the other hand, she might have disposed of it yesterday," George said. "She might have taken it into Allingford and sold it already. Have you made any inquiries into that, Superintendent? Or it might be in her room, if she took one locally. Do you know if she did?"

"We know that she went to The Barley Mow in Oldenham and asked them if they had a room," the Superintendent said, "so it looks as if she'd hoped to stay, but they'd

no room free. We don't know yet where she went after
that, though we shall soon find out."

"When do you want my husband and me to identify
her?" I asked.

"The sooner the better," the Superintendent said. "Not
that it's a case of identifying her. It's only to say if she's the
woman you saw in this house yesterday morning."

"Then let's get it over," I said. "Is she very—very muti-
lated or anything? I'm hoping I don't pass out on your
hands."

I have never fainted in my life, but I have a certain fear
that sooner or later it is bound to happen to me, though I
have never been quite able to imagine what the experience
is like.

He gave me a thoughtful look and said that he did not
think that I should find the woman's appearance unduly
disturbing, apart from the simple fact that she was dead. I
turned to Felix, who said that he agreed with me that the
sooner we could do as the police wished the better.

There is no need for me to describe what happened
next, the drive into Allingford in the police car, the visit
to the mortuary, the sight of the body there, the drawing
back of the covering over the woman's face, and the immediate response from Felix and me that this was certainly
the woman whom we had seen so briefly in the library the
day before. We were shown the clothes that she had been
wearing when she had been found in the white Mini, a
pink silk suit and a frilly white blouse, all thickly stained
with blood, and we stated that so far as we could tell,
these were the clothes that the woman had been wearing.

The sight of these things seemed to upset Felix more
than the sight of the dead face. He had always been a
good deal upset by the sight of blood, and when he had to
look at the stains he took me firmly by the arm, as if to

support me in case I felt the faintness coming on of which I had spoken, but it was really to steady himself. I simply felt a fearful sense of cold, as if it had somehow got into my bones, and afterwards in the police car once more, being driven back to Oldenham, such nausea came on that I was afraid for a time that I might actually be sick. But we arrived at the house without any disaster happening.

As soon as we got out of the car I said to Felix that I wanted to talk to him in private and that I thought we might go to his room in the bungalow. He nodded and we set off together round the house.

As soon as we reached his room he put his suitcase on the bed, opened it, and started to throw things into it. I sat down on the only chair in the room.

"Where are you thinking of going?" I asked.

"I thought we might go to your house, if you've no objection," he said.

"I'd like to go, but don't you think we ought to stay?"

"We're no use, are we? This is a family affair."

"Is that woman we've just seen part of the family?"

He did not answer, but folded a shirt and added it to what was already in the suitcase.

"Felix, you know who she is, don't you?" I said.

He sat down on the edge of the bed, lit a cigarette, and seemed to retire into his own thoughts.

"Well, don't you?" I said. "Why was your telephone number in her notebook?"

"I'm not sure," he answered.

"All the same, you think you know. And the police are going to want to know more about it, aren't they?"

"I suppose so."

"And it's not just because of that number that I think you know something about her. There was the way you looked when you heard her name was Margaret Macinnes.

And there was something too when the General was talking and asked us if we thought she could be American,
and you answered that we hadn't heard her say a word,
and then you suddenly stopped as if you'd just thought of
something. Perhaps there was nothing in it, but I noticed
it at the time."

"You notice too damn much," Felix muttered. "If we
saw more of each other I'd have no private life at all."

"Well, was there anything in it?" I asked. "I mean about
her possibly being American?"

"Nothing whatever."

"I'm sure there was."

"She wasn't American."

"Then why did that question of General Searle's sort of
take you aback?"

"Simply because it made me think of her having some
sort of special accent, and for some reason the thought of
a Scots accent popped into my head, and when that happened I felt as if I almost knew who she was. Only her hair
was the wrong colour and her spectacles changed her face
very much, so I didn't think much more about it."

"Yet when you found she'd a Scottish name it meant
something definite to you."

"Well, yes."

"Who is she?"

He sighed as if he were finding me an intolerable nuisance, which no doubt he was.

"I can't remember if I ever told you that at the time
when I used to see a good deal of Andrew and Paul and
David and Sonia they'd another friend who used to come
with them to Little Carbery Street, but who didn't stay
around long?"

"Christine mentioned her to me," I said. "She said she
faded out."

"Well, that girl came from Glasgow and her name was Margaret McNair."

"Not Macinnes?"

"No, I think that must have been the name of her husband. She was rather a beauty and I was inclined to think both David and Paul were a bit in love with her."

"But then she got married?"

"I think so. I think that's why she faded out. I never knew anything about her husband, but no doubt he came from Glasgow too and the two of them went back there."

"And her hair wasn't blonde and she didn't need spectacles."

"As far as I can remember her hair was an ordinary sort of brown and she certainly didn't wear glasses."

"Felix, don't you think you ought to tell all this to the police?"

He stubbed his cigarette out in the ash-tray by the bed and lit another.

"Honestly, I'm not sure of any of it. I think she may have been the girl who used to be a friend of the others. That would explain how she's still got my telephone number. And if I tell the police what I think, they're going to start putting extra pressure on David and Paul. And on Sonia. Have you thought of that? The police have said the murder could have been done by a woman, and who could have got hold of that knife as easily as Sonia? But I suppose you're right, I'll have to tell them."

Thirteen _____

UPSTAIRS IN MY ROOM, I started to pack my suitcase. Before it was done Christine came in. She gave a little sigh and dropped into the easy chair in the room.

"So you're leaving us," she said, then added inconsequently, "You haven't had any lunch. I'll get Martha to send you up a sandwich."

"Don't bother," I said. "I'll have something when I get home. And the fact is, I've got to get back to work tomorrow."

"Then you could wait till tomorrow, couldn't you? But I understand that you want to leave. It's only natural. What are you doing with Felix?"

"He's coming with me. But if you really want me to stay, Christine, of course I will. It's just that I don't see what use the two of us can be to you."

"Perhaps you can't be." She leant wearily back, pushing back her long fair hair, which was not in its usual neat roll but fell loosely to her shoulders. "Sonia and David have been taken to have a look at that woman in the mortuary. Did she really mean nothing to you when you saw her, Virginia?"

I told her the truth. "Only that she was certainly the woman we saw for a minute in the library." I did not feel inclined to tell her what Felix had had to say about her. "Why have Sonia and David gone? Do they think they can identify her?"

"It was an idea of Sonia's, something to do with her being a Scot, that it might be someone they used to know but hadn't seen for a long time. But even if that's who she was, it doesn't seem to tell us anything about why she came here or why she got herself killed. Perhaps she came because she was in trouble of some sort and thought Sonia and David could help her. But that doesn't explain her murder. Virginia, don't you think I've always been an extraordinarily lucky woman?"

That took me by surprise and, looking at her slumped in the chair, pale and tired, though with the elegance that never left her, I found it difficult to agree.

"Is that what you really feel?" I asked.

"Well, yes, but only when I think seriously about it," she replied. "I've been feeling so sorry for myself all day because of Andrew and because of getting involved in this other strange affair at such a tragic time, and the police here and everything, but the truth is I've had more than my share of good luck and I ought to hold on to that. I've had George all these years. Sometimes when I think of that I almost want to sit and cry. We've been so happy together and when I think of other people who've never had anything of the sort . . . I'm sorry, I'm not talking about you and Felix, I know you've worked things out pretty well to your own satisfaction. But all the same, when I think of the way Andrew and Sonia muddled things up between them, when they might have been so happy together, and then this strange woman in pink having lost her husband and perhaps having started to do strange things because of the shock, and other people I know who've either lost husbands or wives by death or divorce, I think to myself, my God, I'm so lucky, I've got George. . . ." She broke off.

I was not sure if she simply wanted to go on talking or to burst into tears. In the event, she did neither. She turned in her chair so that she could gaze out of one of the windows and seemed to lose herself in bewildering thoughts.

I put my washing things into their plastic bag and put it into my suitcase, then added my brush and comb and the spare pair of shoes that I had brought. My packing is always haphazard and unskilled, but I had brought so little with me that it did not seem to matter. I pulled the lid of the case up and pressed it down to close it.

As if the click of the lock roused her, Christine suddenly said, "Why had that woman got Felix's telephone number in her notebook, d'you know?"

I did not want to tell her, but did not want to tell a downright lie.

"Felix knows such an extraordinary lot of people," I said. "She's probably someone he met sometime."

"Do you think she could have come here to see him?"

"If she did, why did she run away the moment they came face to face?"

"Perhaps because you were with him."

"You aren't suggesting, are you, that he might have murdered her?"

"No, of course not. Well, no, I suppose not. I hadn't really thought of that." She was staring at me as if I had put a new thought into her mind, and I wished very much that I had not spoken. "No, of course not," she repeated firmly, but I saw that the thought had taken root. "Actually I'd be absolutely sure it was someone she picked up in her car—one hears of such awful things being done to people by complete strangers—if it wasn't that the knife seems to have come from here. Do you think that just possibly could be a mistake? I mean, that set of knives probably came from some ironmonger in Allingford and is quite ordinary. It could just be coincidence that the one Mrs. Grantly gave Sonia is missing, don't you think so?"

"I know the most fantastic coincidences happen," I said.

"But you don't believe in this one. All the same, that's what it could be, couldn't it?"

"I imagine the police won't be taking anything for granted. They'll be investigating the purchase of knives like that everywhere in the town."

"If only we could find the knife that's gone missing. Only . . ." She stood up and stretched, giving a desperate yawn. "Of course we won't. I'm not really such a fool as I sound. And I'm so tired. Oh God, I don't believe I've ever felt so tired in my life. And Fran's gone and chosen this time of all times to go and get herself engaged to Paul and she's wild with happiness about it. But the happiness is all being spoilt for her because of Andrew. I don't mean that his death really means so very much to her. She hardly knew him. She'll get over it. But this ought to be a time when she's the centre of everything, being kissed and congratulated and made a fuss of, and instead she's been so horribly let down, poor child. I remember when I got engaged to George we had champagne and my mother sat and wept, she was so pleased about it, and she started talking straight away about my wedding dress."

"Well, perhaps you can have a fine wedding still instead of the one that didn't happen yesterday when Fran marries Paul," I said.

Her face lighted up a little. "So we can! I hadn't thought of that. And it can be the real thing, because I don't think the two of them will have been living together in the meantime. Fran's an absolute innocent, you know, although she's so fond of talking psychology. And you'll come to that wedding, won't you?"

She suddenly put her arms round me and kissed me.

"You always help me so much," she said. "I don't know how you do it."

Nor did I, but I was glad that she thought I did. She left me and I opened my suitcase again because I realised that I had forgotten to put in the one good dress I possessed, which I had brought for the wedding and which was still on its hanger in the wardrobe. When I had folded it and put it into the case I found that it would not close. I had to tumble everything out of it on to the bed and start from the beginning again.

I was in the middle of doing this when Fran came in. For a moment she stood in the doorway, smiling at me with a warmth of which I had seen little in the house that day. I thought how pretty she was, how full of charm and vitality. But perhaps she herself felt that there was something inappropriate about this at the moment, for as she came forward into the room the smile disappeared and a look solemn and a little guilty took its place.

"Isn't it awful, Virginia," she said, "but I feel so happy. I feel I've got everything in the world that I've ever wanted."

"That's a wonderful feeling," I said. "I'd hang on to it as long as I could."

"But with everyone else so wretched, isn't it just beastly selfishness?"

"Perhaps it is, but I wouldn't let that worry me too much."

"It isn't as if I'd ever really known Andrew."

"No."

"But I feel terrible when I think of him, mostly because of Mum and Dad."

"Of course you do. But no doubt it's different when you think of Paul."

"So you know all about it."

"It would have been difficult not to guess what had happened when the two of you came in from the pool. And only a short time ago Christine told me that you were definitely engaged." I folded my dress carefully and put it into my case. "Did you have to ask him to marry you, as you threatened?"

"No, of course I didn't," she said, and the smile broke out again, lighting up her young face like sunshine. "What nonsense I talked to you about that, didn't I? That's why I wanted to come and talk to you when Mum said you were going home. I didn't want you to have any wrong ideas about us. Paul, all in a dither, asked me if I'd think of it, as if he had the slightest reason to doubt it. You know, he's the first person I've ever been seriously in love with."

She sat down in the chair where Christine had been sitting only a short while before, and gave a little laugh of delight.

"Have there been others then, not quite so serious?" I asked.

"Good heavens, yes," she answered. "There was Kurt in Zurich, Ilse's brother, ever so nice, but somehow when it came to the point, well, I just came home. And there was one called Jimmy, but that didn't last long. The most serious, the very first time that I ever fell in love, was when I was about ten years old. I was with some friends at a party and suddenly a boy about my own age ran across the room and knocked me down and I immediately fell in love with him."

"So cave-man tactics sometimes work," I said.

"Yes, indeed. I used to meet him from time to time in the holidays and on and off I went on being in love with him till I was about fifteen."

"Why did he knock you down?" I asked. "Had he anything against you?"

"No, that was the fine thing about it, you see. Just the sight of me gave him this urge. A sort of sexual thing, of course, as my response to it was. But he never really cared for me much. There were other little girls in his life."

"And what happened to him in the end?"

"Oh, I don't know. I've an idea his family went to Australia, or somewhere like that. I grew out of him completely, luckily for me, because I believe I'd have found him an awful bore when I got older. Yet I've always remembered it, isn't it funny?"

I could have told her one or two similar things about myself, but did not think that she would be much interested. It was her own life that she was reviewing in the bright light of her new experience, and of which she was trying to make sense.

"So Paul doesn't mind you being a rich girl," I said.

She gave a quick frown. "I'm not sure that I like the way you said that. I told you everything I said yesterday was nonsense."

"Certainly that's how it sounded to me at the time," I said.

The smile came back. "Yes, I think I realised you weren't taking me very seriously. All the same, when he started to talk about marriage, I did—well, sort of—try to help him along a bit. Then all at once everything was settled and it felt so wonderful. There's just one thing that worries me."

She paused, regarding me thoughtfully. I waited for her to go on and after a moment she did.

"You see, most of the married girls I know experimented

a bit before they actually got around to marrying, and I'm wondering if that isn't the right way to do things. I mean, marriage is a bit of a leap in the dark, isn't it?"

"It is indeed."

"Yet I don't want the sort of thing Sonia and David have had for so long. I want a real marriage from the beginning. Is that stupid of me?"

"I'd hate to give an opinion."

She sighed. "That's what Mum always says about you. She says you never give opinions and that's what makes it so comfortable to talk to you. But isn't it a good idea to have had a little sexual experience before you actually get married?"

"I don't really see how you could organise it now that you and Paul have made your engagement so public," I said. "That's to say, if you don't want everyone to know what you're doing and to be keeping an eye on you."

"Oh, of course I shouldn't want that."

"Then why not risk just going ahead with the marriage, specially if you'd like the grand sort of wedding that Christine yearns for. After all, if it doesn't work out, there's always divorce. It's easy enough nowadays."

"Only I'd hate just to be a statistic," she said.

I was puzzled. "A statistic?"

"Yes, there was a television programme I watched the other day about one-parent families and that sort of thing, and they gave the statistics of how many divorces there are compared with marriages—well, of course I don't mean they said there are more divorces than marriages, that wouldn't have made sense—but all the same, it was a terrible number, though I can't remember what it was. And I don't want to be just one more on the list, even though I believe second marriages sometimes work out very well. But I can't imagine ever wanting to marry anyone after

Paul. But I'm sure this is all awfully boring for you. You'd sooner talk about murder."

"Truly I'm glad to talk about something else," I said, again closing the lid of my suitcase and this time succeeding in shutting it. "I'm grateful to you for reminding me that life goes on."

"Of course you know who did the murder, don't you?" she said.

I looked at her in surprise because her tone had changed. I saw that her small, vivid face was extremely earnest.

"Do you believe you do?" I asked.

She gave a grave nod. "And you really don't?"

"If I did," I said, "I'd have told the police by now."

"Ah, that's where we're different." She stood up and took a few steps towards the door. "But you haven't the same reasons for keeping it to yourself as I have. All the same, I should have thought it was obvious."

I was suddenly anxious for her. "Fran, if there's really something you know, I shouldn't go around talking like that to other people. There's someone about who's already killed two people."

"Not two people, only one," she answered, "and anyway, it happens I'm quite safe."

She went quickly out of the room, leaving me feeling disturbed and astonished.

Before Felix and I said farewell to Christine and George, Sonia and David, who had been taken into Allingford after Felix had spoken to the police, had returned and confirmed what Felix had said about the dead woman. She was someone who had been a friend of theirs at Oxford, though perhaps more of Andrew's than of the rest of them, sharing his determination to succeed in the theatre or on films, but they did not think that she had ever done so, even in a small way. They thought that after a while in London she had gone back to Glasgow, for she had lost all contact with them. Her name had been Margaret Mc-Nair. They presumed that she had married someone called Macinnes, but they knew nothing about that. Why she had come to Oldenham they could not guess.

"What's really very odd about it," Sonia said, just as Felix and I were about to leave, "is that having got here, I suppose to see David and me, she didn't wait to do it. Do you think she'd become a kleptomaniac, couldn't resist that necklace when she saw it, and then realised when she'd taken it that she couldn't stay around to meet us. If that's so, it seems very sad. I mean, what with her having lost her husband recently in a car crash, I think we'd have tried to be understanding. We were all very good friends once."

"It may not have been you and David she came to see," George said. "It seems to me it was probably Andrew. However, that's for the police to work out."

Felix and I said good-bye to the party and went out to our cars, which Bob had driven round from the garages. I drove home with Felix tailing me. When we arrived I drove into my garage and he parked his car in the street in front of the house. Going into it I was almost overcome by my feeling of relief, it felt somehow so safe. It is an undistinguished little house, and it is somewhat too full of furniture of a complete mixture of periods, but I am very fond of it. When the front door closed behind us I realised how over-exposed I had been feeling in the Appleyards' much more beautiful residence, while here I felt peaceful and secure. But the rooms seemed stuffy from the house having been left shut up for the last few days and I went round, opening windows.

Going into the kitchen, I opened my small freezer and took out a packet of tagliatelli with cheese and prawns.

"I don't know about you, but I'm feeling very hungry," I said. That we had missed our lunch was something that I was only beginning to feel now that I was back in my own normal world. "And while this warms up I'm going to have a drink."

"As usual, the first thing you think of," Felix said. The first thing that he had thought of was lighting a cigarette. "All right, I'll get it. What do you want, sherry?"

"Please."

Although he does not live there, he still knows where everything is in my house. While he was fetching the drinks, I put the tagliatelli into the oven, then went to the sitting-room and dropped into a chair. But almost at once I got up again because I had a feeling, looking round the room, that I would like some flowers in it. Taking some scissors with me, I went into the garden and cut half a dozen roses and on returning put them into a vase and took it to the sitting-room. Felix had brought out my Tio Pepe and two glasses and was pouring out drinks.

"Do you know, a queer thing happened before we left Oldenham," I said as I sipped my drink. "Fran told me she quite positively knew who'd done the murders."

"She's so positive about a lot of things," Felix said. "She could be wrong."

"But an odd thing about it was that she said there'd only been one murder."

He raised his eyebrows. "She really said that?"

I did my best to remember just what she had said. "No, actually I've got it wrong, she didn't. What I said was that if she really knew anything she shouldn't talk about it to all and sundry, because there was someone about who'd already killed two people, and she said no, only one."

"Oh, I see," he said, as if that explained everything.

"Do you know what she probably meant?" I asked.

"I can make a fair guess," he answered.

"Well, what was it?"

"She didn't tell you herself whom she suspected?"

"No, and when I told her she ought to tell the police if she really knew anything, she said I hadn't the same sort of reason for keeping it quiet as she had. And that I suppose means that she thinks it's one of the family, because she also said she was quite safe. But which of them does she think it was, for heaven's sake? Don't tell me she suspects either of her parents."

"No, I shouldn't think so. In my view it's fairly obvious. I've even toyed with the idea myself, but I can see one serious thing against it."

"Are you going to tell me about this idea of yours, or are you planning to keep it to yourself?"

"Well, who could it be but the General?"

"General Searle?" I was startled and shocked.

"Yes, naturally General Searle. There aren't any other generals around, are there? And you see, when he was a young man he was a commando and has probably done his share of killing in the dark, perhaps even of stabbing in the neck. I don't for a minute believe he killed his own grandson, but if he knew that the Macinnes girl had done it, or even if he merely believed it without any real evidence, he might have killed her in revenge. And that's what Fran meant when she said that whoever she suspected had done only one murder. According to her theory the first murderer Margaret Macinnes is dead already, so that leaves only one at large."

Fourteen _____

"YOU SAY YOU'VE TOYED with Fran's idea yourself," I said, "but that you can see something serious against it. I can see several things, the main one being the character of General Searle, even if he was once a commando. But what's your special objection to it?"

"Isn't it a fact that he suffers rather badly from arthritis?" Felix said.

"Yes, poor man. But it's in his knees. It wouldn't stop him stabbing someone in the neck."

"No, but it might stop him walking all the way from Reservoir Lane back to Oldenham House. That would be rather an undertaking."

I thought it over.

"It isn't very far," I said.

"Not for you or me. But for someone whose knees hurt him like hell once he does a little walking, it'd be quite a distance."

"I suppose so."

"The arthritis is genuine, is it?"

"Oh yes, he's been to the clinic to see if we could help him, but what he really needs is an operation. But you know, this is too absurd."

"What is?"

"Thinking we could work out whether or not the General could be a murderer according to the amount of pain he'd get in his knees. It's the man himself you've got to think about. And killing enemy soldiers in the dark in Occupied France when there's a war on, if he ever really did that, is quite different from killing a young woman in a Mini in Reservoir Lane, Oldenham."

"Even if he was sure she'd done a murder?"

"Even then. He'd hand whatever evidence he had over to the police. I'm sure he's very law-abiding."

"Well, of course I agree with you. But I wanted to know what you'd think about it. After all, he's a very tough old boy. If he'd really wanted to undertake that walk, however much it hurt him, he'd have done it."

"No, it just won't do."

"All right then, no. We must think of something else."

I went to the kitchen to see how the tagliatelli was getting on.

It was about half-past six when the doorbell rang. When I went to answer it I found Detective Superintendent Dawnay and Sergeant Wells on the doorstep. The Superintendent apologized for disturbing me, asked me if it was correct that my husband was here, and said that there were just a few things which he thought we might be able to help him clear up. I took him and the sergeant into the sitting-room, offered them both drinks, and was only mildly shocked when they accepted.

Felix gave both of them the beer they asked for, then said, "I think the Superintendent's just going to ask me about why Margaret Macinnes had my telephone number in her notebook."

"Ah, I thought that was probably it," I said.

"But Mr. Freer hasn't answered that question yet," the

Superintendent said. "I'd be grateful if you could clear that little matter up, Mr. Freer."

"As a matter of fact, it surprised me a little when I heard of it," Felix said. "I don't think I've seen her for four or five years. I shouldn't have thought she'd keep a note of my number all that time."

"But you used to know her?"

"Oh yes, I believe she even stayed in my flat once or twice. She was one of that group who were friends at Oxford, Appleyard, Eldred, Camrose, and Sonia Capel. They used to find my flat rather a convenience when they happened to want to spend a night in London—not so comfortable as a hotel, but much cheaper."

"But you said nothing about that when you saw her body in the mortuary."

"No, I didn't, did I?" It was as if the thought of that now surprised Felix. "The fact is, I wasn't sure. As I told you, it's a long time since I last saw her, and then she was —well, she was alive. That makes a difference, you know. There was always plenty of colour in her face, most of it real, and the way I remember her, she was usually laughing, which somehow made her face a different face. When I saw that woman in the morgue—well, it wasn't only that she was older than the one I remembered, but it was quite terribly like the ghost of her, if you know what I mean, not the real woman at all. So although I got a sort of shiver up my spine when I saw her, I couldn't for the moment have sworn I knew her. I'm sorry if it's given you any trouble."

The Superintendent gave a slight shrug of his shoulders, as if he was so used to trouble of that sort that this hardly counted.

"There's something besides your number that we found

in Mrs. Macinnes's handbag, which is of some interest," he said. "Will you take a look at this?"

He took a wallet out of a pocket, extracted from it what looked like a letter, and handed it to Felix.

"It's a photocopy," the detective said. "The original's back at the station."

"Is this another forgery?" Felix unfolded the paper and looked down at it.

"I haven't the least idea," the Superintendent answered. "Perhaps you can help us with that."

"How am I supposed to do that?" Felix asked. "It's typewritten."

"Sometimes that can tell one a great deal." The Superintendent looked at me. "Have you a typewriter, Mrs. Freer?"

I do not believe I have ever seen Felix look so angry. He held out the paper to me.

"Read this before you answer," he said.

I took it and read. It had no address or signature.

"No! Don't try anything like that with me, Maggie. Perhaps I'll give you some help if I can, but not if you threaten me. Remember I've something on you and you've nothing on me, except that I've kept quiet about what you did. Haven't I kept quiet all this time? You ought to be grateful. If later you think you've something on me, don't think I won't protect myself. If you try to dig up evidence about me, you'll only incriminate yourself. And who are you going to use for witnesses? The old boy who came in off the street? He's dead, I checked that. And the other wouldn't be interested. Here's £100, and if you're really in trouble at the moment, I'll help a bit, but don't expect too much. Use your talents to get on your own feet and keep out of my way. That's good advice. Take it."

I read this twice, then handed it back to the Superintendent.

"There's a typewriter on that desk behind you," I said. "Do you want to try it?"

He looked a little sheepish. "I wasn't seriously accusing you of having written this, Mrs. Freer. I don't think that would make sense."

"All the same, try it."

"Does anyone else ever have a chance to use it, if you don't mind my asking?"

"If you mean me," Felix said in a dangerously quiet tone, "yes, I've sometimes done so. I also have a typewriter at home. If you like I'll give you a key to my flat in London and you can go and test it."

"Thank you," the Superintendent said. "We may do that."

"Anyway, please check my typewriter now," I said. I knew its type was quite different from that of the letter. "I realise you've got to explore every avenue—"

"Those bloody avenues again!" Felix interrupted me.

"Please go ahead, Superintendent," I said. "Then perhaps you can tell us what you think that letter means."

"Thank you," he said, stood up, and turned to the writing-table on which my very old Adler stood.

There was a pile of typing paper beside it. He slid a sheet into the machine, typed a few lines, then extracted the paper, crumpled it, and tossed it into the waste paper basket beside the desk. He turned to me with a faintly sardonic smile.

"One of the avenues that didn't lead anywhere," he said. "I confess I didn't expect it to."

"But are you going to tell us what this letter means?" I asked.

"We don't know any more about it than you do," he

answered. "We've had a little more time to think about it, but all we've come up with is guesswork. To begin with, when is it most likely that someone will be brought in off the street to be a witness to something? Isn't it a marriage? Don't people have a way of turning up at registry offices without the necessary witnesses, expecting to find someone there to act for them or to be able to persuade someone to come in from outside and sign on the line?"

"But we know Margaret Macinnes was married," Felix said. "I know marriage is going out of fashion, but it isn't actually illegal, is it? Because that's what you've suggested and what this letter implies. The Macinnes woman was trying to blackmail someone who knew about her marriage."

"It isn't illegal if you stick to one at a time," the Superintendent said, "but bigamy is still a criminal offence."

"Bigamy! So that's what's at the bottom of it all, is it?"

"I tell you, this is only guesswork, but isn't it how the letter reads to you?"

"May I see it again?" Felix held out his hand for it.

The Superintendent gave the letter back to him and Felix read it, frowned, then returned it to the other man.

"I think I agree with you," Felix said. "Mrs. Macinnes, if that's what we still call her, even if she had a former husband in existence and hadn't bothered with the formality of a divorce, knew that that husband, the writer of that letter, was going to get married again himself and she tried a little quiet blackmail. After all, the man couldn't simply divorce her and go ahead with his second marriage legally because he's connived at her bigamy, and even if the law wouldn't take that too seriously, his second wife might not have liked it. But who's this witness to the first marriage who wouldn't be interested in the situation? The other one, who obliged by coming into the registry office as he was passing by, is dead, but it sounds as if the other's still living. Who is he?"

"I wouldn't swear to it that he's still living," the Superintendent said.

"You mean—no, you don't, or do you?" I broke in. "It was Andrew Appleyard."

He looked uneasy. "That's going a bit fast, Mrs. Freer, but well, it had crossed my mind as a possibility."

"But in that case . . ."

Felix took up my unfinished sentence. "In that case, aren't you almost accusing David Eldred of having murdered Appleyard?"

"It does give him a motive, doesn't it?" the Superintendent said. "I mean, apart from that other motive we've been considering, that Eldred knew Appleyard was planning to murder him."

"So you've been talking to Sonia Capel," Felix said.

The Superintendent looked puzzled. "I don't quite understand that."

"She hasn't told you her theory that Appleyard was intending to murder Eldred?"

"No, I thought of that all by myself." A faint grin appeared on the detective's face. "Sometimes I do that."

Felix sighed. "I shouldn't have spoken."

"If you'd care to tell me what you mean. . . ."

"Oh, it was only something she said to my wife and me yesterday. She said that the letters in Appleyard's room, the one that is definitely in his writing and that says he was killing himself because he realised his love for her was hopeless, and the few lines of the other which was on his lap, were part of a plot to kill Eldred in a way that was to look like suicide. The first complete letter was a draft of what he meant to say, then the second, in which he was forging Eldred's handwriting, was the one that some time or other was to be left by Eldred's body, after he'd apparently shot himself with Appleyard's gun. When she talked about this I pointed out to her that that gave Eldred a motive for killing Appleyard, but she claimed that it didn't, as Eldred couldn't have known what was in Appleyard's mind. And on the whole that seemed to make sense to me."

The Superintendent nodded. "I think she was probably right that Eldred didn't know that Appleyard had murder in mind."

"But do you think he really had?" Felix asked.

"I believe so. It's the only way I can make sense of those two letters. What we don't know, and what I suppose we'll never know, is how serious he was about carrying it out. At some time he must have practiced forging Eldred's writing, so the thought of something of the kind must have been in his mind before he came here. But it could have been just a kind of fantasy, something he'd never really have done. Then the sight of Eldred and Miss Capel together and knowing they were going to get married next day, and for all we know that bang on the head he had when he fell when he was filming, may have sparked something off so that he kidded himself he'd really get around to doing it sometime. So he settled down to write that letter, not knowing, of course, that he himself was on the way out. By the way, it wasn't the Somnolin that killed him."

"It *wasn't!*" I said, unbelieving.

"No, it made him unconscious, but what finished him off was a pillow held over his face. The forensic people found that."

"So the murderer did come twice to his room," Felix said. "I'd thought of that because of the way the forged

letter was lying beside him when he'd settled down to
write his own forged letter.

"That's right. And enough Somnolin to have killed
him, even taken in brandy, would have tasted strange. So
he was given enough to knock him out, then his visitor
came back to finish the job and leave the forged letter
about his illness behind."

"When Appleyard was in a deep sleep. One can hardly
call it the sleep of the just—rather of the unjust, if he was
really plotting murder himself."

"But that forged letter couldn't have been knocked off
in a few minutes, you know," the Superintendent said. "A
thing like that takes care and skill. So whoever wrote it
needed a fair bit of time to prepare it."

"So he knew that Appleyard was coming here, even
though no one's admitted expecting him, is that what
you're leading up to?" Felix asked.

"And it happens that Appleyard arrived in this country
on Thursday afternoon, not Friday, and he went to your
flat and inquired of one of your neighbours if she knew
where you were. She said she thought you were at home,
as she'd seen you come in only a short time before." The
Superintendent spoke in a tone of quiet detachment. "Can
you explain that?"

I have very seldom seen Felix's face turn blank. He has a
very expressive face, even though what it expresses may
not always be what is going on in his mind. But for an
instant now it was totally blank. Then a look of interest
appeared in his eyes.

"So that was it," he said.

"You were at home when Appleyard called?" the Superintendent asked.

"Well, I presume it was him, since you say he came,"
Felix said. "I heard the bell ring, but I didn't answer it."

"Why not?"

"Because I was having a bath."

"I see, do you often have baths in the afternoon?"

"Quite often. I have no regular time for the operation."

"But you heard the bell ring?"

"Yes."

"How often?"

"I'm not sure. Two or three times. In fact, once he kept his finger on the bell for so long that I began to think he was really impatient and it might be something important, though I couldn't think what, and I very nearly got out of my bath to answer the damned thing, but then he went away."

"And what did you do then?"

"Well, naturally I eventually got out of the bath, got dressed, packed a suitcase, and drove down to Oldenham." Felix gave one of the smiles which I usually found charming, but which now I thought of as faintly sinister. It meant that he felt that he was a step ahead of the rest of us and was going to have one of his private jokes. "I can't prove any of this, except that I arrived at the Appleyards' in time for dinner and it takes about an hour and a half, driving only moderately fast, as I normally do, to reach them from my flat in London. But that I didn't see Andrew Appleyard in the afternoon, that he didn't tell me he was going to visit his parents, so giving me time to prepare the forged letter before I set off, is something I can't prove. However, if by any chance you believe me, can you tell me where he spent the night?"

The Superintendent shook his head. "Not yet."

"Could he have spent it with Margaret Macinnes?"

"It's possible, though we've no evidence that he did. But can you tell us, Mr. Freer, why he should have come to you at all? He was a successful and I assume fairly wealthy man. Wouldn't the normal thing for him to have done on arriving in London after several years abroad have been to go to a hotel, a rather good one?"

"I'm sure it's what I'd have done myself," Felix answered, "if you're ready to accept that what I'd be likely to do in any given circumstances should be accepted as normal. But there was a time, you see, when Appleyard used to doss down in my flat quite often. He and a group of his friends used to find it very convenient to stay there if they'd come to London to go to a theatre, or a party, or a political gathering of some sort, or something like that. So on suddenly getting home from America after all those years, I think he may have been overcome by a wave of nostalgia, sheer homesickness, or what have you, and thought he'd like to try to recapture something of those old days when he was young and hopeful and the thought of murder would have seemed utterly fantastic. Perhaps he even wanted to confide in me. We used to get on very well. He may half have hoped I'd talk him out of what he had in mind. Why the bloody hell did I have that bath?"

"This is all guesswork, of course," the Superintendent said.

"Oh, entirely," Felix agreed. "I'm just doing what I can to answer your questions. Have you any more?"

"Only one, and it isn't exactly a question." The Superintendent stood up as if he were preparing to leave. The sergeant stood up too. "You've been very helpful, but perhaps there's one thing more you can tell me. You can guess, of course, that we found your fingerprints in the room Appleyard slept in on Friday night."

"Yes," Felix said. "I was in there in the morning we found him."

"And we've found his father's and his mother's and his grandfather's and the doctor's. But we've also found those of Mr. Eldred and Mr. Camrose, and they didn't go into the room that morning. Can you tell me anything about why they should be there?"

"That's simple. They both kept their swimming things in that room and I believe changed there when they were going to swim."

"Ah yes, Mrs. Appleyard told me that. Now why didn't I remember?"

I was quite sure that the Superintendent had remembered and had only asked the question to see if he would trip up either Felix or Christine. But they had both given him the same answer.

He turned towards the door, then paused. "I don't believe I've told you that we've found the missing necklace."

"No," Felix said. "Where was it?"

"In the lady's handbag, along with her notebook."

"So robbery wasn't the motive for her murder," I said, remembering my own flimsy idea that it might have been.

"No, apparently not."

The two detectives left.

We were both silent for a little while after they had gone, then Felix said, "What are we going to have for supper? I fancy an omelette."

"In that case, you can make it," I said. Felix makes much better omelettes than I do.

"All right," he said. "But you do realise something, don't you, Virginia? That man came here with the idea at the back of his mind that I might be a forger and a murderer. And I wouldn't swear to it that it isn't in his mind still, and not so far to the back of it. To be honest with you, I did once forge a friend's cheque, but only because she was too drunk to sign it herself and we were running out of ready cash. All I had to do was scribble an indecipherable signature and put in a few figures."

"I wonder how much the cheque was for," I said.

"I've forgotten. Not more than two or three hundred anyway."

"Oh, an insignificant amount!"

"Well, isn't it, these days? Once upon a time I'd have lived on it for six months, but now it's gone in a flash."

"What about that omelette?"

"Yes, yes, I'll see to it." He moved towards the door.

"And, Felix—"

"Yes?"

"Whatever else I've ever suspected you of, it's never been murder. I find that idea totally improbable and unconvincing. I'm sure you would never be capable of it."

"D'you know, I believe that's the nicest thing you've ever said to me," he replied with that puzzling and faintly sinister little smile back on his face. "I'll treasure the memory. Now I wonder if you've any mushrooms for that omelette, or would you prefer cheese?"

Fifteen

NEXT MORNING I went to the clinic and did not return until nearly one o'clock. I found Felix seated at my dining-table, busily writing something. There were several sheets of paper spread out before him, covered with his neat script, and it was a moment after I had come into the room before he interrupted himself to look up and say, "Hallo."

"What are you doing?" I asked.

"Just a bit of work," he answered. "I thought I might as well get ahead with it while you were away. I've helped myself to some paper out of your desk. I hope you don't mind."

"What sort of work would that be?"

"Just one of my articles for *The Grail.*"

I had completely forgotten that he had told me that he occasionally wrote travel articles for *The Grail.*

"And just where have you been wandering, fancy free, this morning?" I asked. "Africa, China, the Antipodes?"

"No, as a matter of fact, only in the Hebrides," he said.

"But you've actually been there," I said. "We once went to Mull together, and you insisted on going all the way up the Sound, instead of the short way by ferry, and you were horribly sick all the way."

"Yes, I remember I thought it would be picturesque and it never occurred to me how rough it could be. Of course what I've described is the trip by ferry, as that's what most people do now. Actually I was planning on doing something about Malawi, but I've left the necessary references at home. But about this paper . . ."

"You're welcome to it."

"Thanks, but that wasn't what I was about to ask. I wanted to know, was there any notepaper in your bedroom at Oldenham?"

"No, I don't think so. I can't say I looked for any, but there was nothing in the way of a writing-table in my room."

"Nor there was in mine."

"What about it?"

"It's not very important, it's just something I'd like cleared up. I don't think there was any in Andrew's room either, and when I did my quick scout around the house in search of pills, I didn't find any paper that matched what that forged letter was written on. The one about Andrew's incurable illness. And that indicates that the letter wasn't written in that house, but was taken there ready prepared, which means, of course, that it was written by someone who knew he was going to Oldenham, and that could have been someone with whom he stayed the night, or at least spent the evening with when he found he couldn't get hold of me." He began to pile his sheets of paper together. "You know, Virginia, I find it terribly upsetting to think that if I hadn't taken it into my head to have a bath that afternoon, perhaps two murders wouldn't have happened."

He did look truly upset.

To try to console him, I said, "They might not have happened this week-end, but I suspect they'd have happened sometime. That's to say, I'm not sure if the murder of Margaret Macinnes would or not. It may have been a matter of impulse. But I'm certain Andrew's wasn't. It was a very carefully thought out thing, and if he'd somehow escaped with his life that evening, it would have happened some other time."

He nodded. "I suppose that's right. But now let's go out to lunch. And afterwards I'm going up to London. Do you want to come with me?"

"Why? Where are you going?"

I did not want to go to the flat in Little Carbery Street. I very seldom go there. For a short time I had been so wonderfully happy in it, and afterwards, for a rather longer time, so desolate that I prefer to avoid the fearful mixture of emotions that it arouses in me. But Felix knew this and was unlikely to be inviting me to go there.

"I thought of paying a call on David's flat in Fulham," he said. "Of course, if it's overflowing with police we'll quietly drive on, but it could be interesting to know if he's got a typewriter and any of the kind of paper that both the letters to Andrew and to Margaret Macinnes were written on."

"But he won't be there, so how are you going to get in?"

He gave me a pitying look and I ought to have known better than to ask the question. There are not many ordinary locks that defeat Felix. Of course he cannot do much about any really sophisticated system of security, but he once had a burglar friend who taught him all that he knew about how to go to work with a piece of plastic, and I thought it unlikely, as plainly he did himself, that David and Sonia would have any very complicated lock on their door.

"As a matter of fact," he said as he stood up, "I'm almost certain he's got a typewriter. I've been to the flat and I think I remember seeing one. It's the paper I'm interested in. If we find there's some of what looks like the right kind and we type a few lines on it, we can show it to our detective friend and see how it matches up with the letters he's got in his keeping."

"So you really believe David was about to commit bigamy when he married Sonia, and murdered Andrew because he knew it! Andrew was that other witness to David's original marriage who was supposed not to be too much interested in the whole thing, but when he turned up to see David on Thursday evening after visiting you, showed that he was very interested indeed. So interested that Andrew started to make plans to murder David. Is that it?"

"I'm just exploring one of those avenues," Felix said.

"And suppose it leads up to a brick wall."

"Then we'll have had a trip to London and when we get back we might end up with a good dinner in The Rose and Crown."

The Rose and Crown is Allingford's best hotel and restaurant. If Felix was thinking of giving me dinner there, then his travel articles must be bringing him in more than I should have expected, or else his former Arab employer must have paid him very handsomely. On the other hand, it was always possible that when we got to the restaurant it would turn out that he had left his wallet at home, so as always when I went out with him, I made sure before we set out that I had enough money in my handbag to cover all eventualities. If it turned out that I had not, we might have to be satisfied with a drink in the bar and come home to something out of the freezer. However, I had cashed a cheque fairly recently, and thought that even if Felix had less than he imagined we should be able to eat in reasonable luxury.

We had a lunch of sandwiches and coffee at one of the service stations on the motorway to London and arrived at the flat which David and Sonia had been occupying for the last two years at about half past two. It was in a block of flats of the late Edwardian period and theirs was on the second floor. We met no one going up the stone stairs to it. I have never made a practice of breaking and entering and I found myself drawing uncomfortably short breaths as we mounted. When we reached the door Felix rang the bell twice in case we had somehow miscalculated and Sonia and David, or at least one of them, had come home. But there was no answer to his ringing or any sound of movement in the flat. Taking his precious piece of plastic out of his pocket, he went to work on the lock, and in about two minutes we were inside.

The flat consisted of a living-room, a bedroom, a bathroom, and a little kitchen. It was somewhat austerely furnished with light-coloured modern furniture and easy chairs of the steel and plastic kind. There was a single large very abstract painting on one wall of the living-room. The only untidiness in the whole flat was in that room on a table in front of one of the windows. It was covered with a jumble of books, papers, and notebooks. Also there was a typewriter on it.

Felix went to it and stood looking down at it thoughtfully without touching it.

After a moment he said, "This is an Adler, like yours, but the type may be different. We'll try it."

But he did not help himself immediately to a sheet of the typing paper in a box on the table. Instead, turning, he went to a closed bureau in a corner of the room and, opening it, found notepaper in a pigeon-hole inside it. But this had a letter-head which neither the forged letter found in Andrew's room nor the one in Margaret Macinnes's handbag had had. Of course the letter-head might simply have been cut off both of them, and the colour and the texture did not tell us much. However, Felix was not ready to leave the matter there.

He went carefully through every drawer in the bureau before finally closing it and shaking his head. He then went into the bedroom and found there what looked like a small writing-table, but this, with a standing mirror on it, had been converted into a dressing-table and its drawers contained only cosmetics, some jewellery, and a box of tissues. He tried the kitchen and the bathroom too, with no success. In the bathroom he opened a small wall-cupboard above the basin and examined carefully some bottles of pills that he found there.

"No Somnolin," he said as he closed the cupboard.

"So we might as well be going home," I said.

"I think I'll just check the typewriter first," he said.

We returned to the living-room and he slid a sheet of typing paper into the typewriter and typed out a few words. It intrigued me that the words he chose were the first words of the letter that had been found in Margaret Macinnes's handbag.

"No! Don't try anything like that with me, Maggie. . . ."

I recognised them, though I had not remembered them.

"Well?" I said.

"No," he answered. He pulled the paper out of the typewriter, crumpled it, and thrust it into his pocket. Turning, he looked round the room. "We haven't left any signs of having been here, have we?"

"No doubt a good collection of finger-prints," I said.

"I don't suppose that will matter."

"Did you really expect to find anything, Felix?" I asked.

"Not exactly, but we have found something."

"Oh, you mean something negative. We found that David almost certainly didn't write either of the letters."

"Well, we can say he probably didn't write them here. But he might have typed the one on the quiet in Arne Webster."

"In Allingford, d'you mean?"

"That's where David mostly worked, isn't it?"

"So we're now going to make a raid on it and insist on investigating their stationery and testing all their typewriters. And of course they'll be so glad to cooperate."

He ignored my sarcasm.

"No, we're going somewhere else, as we're in London. Paul's got a flat in South Kensington."

"Paul? Whyever Paul? I thought we'd agreed he hadn't a motive, at least for Andrew's murder, whatever the Macinnes woman may have had on him."

"It's true he hadn't any motive for Andrew's murder at the time it happened. Let's just say that he knew he was going to acquire a motive."

"A motive for a murder that had been done already?"

"Yes, exactly that. In any case, let's get going."

We had come in Felix's car and he was driving. I am terrified of driving in London, but he is so accustomed to it that he treats it with deceptive casualness. It led me, when we had gone only a little way, moving at the snail's pace that cannot be avoided in the clogged traffic, to try to talk to him, only to be told not to distract him when he was trying to concentrate. I thought that this was really only because he had not made up his mind what he wanted to say about this desire of his to visit Paul's flat, and we had reached it before I tried again.

"What you mean is that Andrew, alive, might have interfered with something Paul intended to do in the future."

"You can put it like that if you want to," Felix said.

"But what's put that into your head?"

"Mostly what Ilse said."

"Ilse?" I was puzzled.

We had had to park some way from the block of flats where Paul lived and were walking towards it.

"Yes, don't you remember what she told us about the behaviour of the woman in pink when she heard that the wedding was off?"

"She told us she swore."

"But what did she actually say?"

"She said, 'What wedding?' "

"No, she didn't, she said, 'Which wedding?' "

"Is that important? Wasn't it just Ilse's bad English?"

"I don't think so. I think it was what the woman said."

"So she was expecting some other wedding to be happening that morning."

"That's how it sounds to me. And she swore because if it had been Paul who had been intending to get married that day it would have added to her power over him. It was quite a disappointment to her to find that it wasn't on the cards, and for all she knew, never would be."

We had reached the entrance to the block of flats which we had been approaching. It was rather more luxurious than the one in which David and Sonia lived. It had a thickly carpeted hall, a lift, and a porter. Felix walked confidently towards the lift, showing that he knew where he was going, but all the same the porter emerged from his little office to ask us whom we wanted. When Felix answered that we were calling on Mr. Camrose, the porter said that he believed Mr. Camrose was not in.

All innocence, Felix inquired, "Has he been away long? I tried to phone him on Thursday evening and couldn't get an answer."

"Oh, he was home Thursday evening," the porter said, "though come to think of it, he and his friend may have gone out to dinner. But he didn't go off for the week-end till Friday morning early."

"And he hasn't come back yet?" Felix asked.

"Not as I knows of," the porter said, "though I suppose he might have gone up without my seeing him. Was he expecting you?"

"Yes, I think so," Felix lied.

"Shall I phone up for you and see if he's there?"

"No, please don't trouble. We'll just go up and see if he's in. Number Twelve, isn't it?"

"That's right." The porter seemed to be accepting us as respectable friends of Paul's who might be admitted. "Second floor."

Felix took me by the arm, as if he was going to guide me to the lift, but then he lingered.

"By the way, the friend who was with Mr. Camrose on Thursday evening, was he that actor Jon Sanchez?" he asked.

"Come to think of it, I believe it was," the porter answered, looking interested. "I thought he looked kind of familiar, though I couldn't have put a name to him. Don't go much to the films myself. Famous man, is he?"

"Fairly so, I believe. Well, thank you for your help."

The information that Andrew had probably spent Thursday night here was perhaps worth the thanks, but it made me feel curiously queasy. As Felix and I went up in the lift I had a kind of feeling that is unusual for me, a sense for which I could not account that we were approaching something horrifying and evil. I am not an intuitive person and can very rarely claim to have experienced forebodings or to be specially sensitive to atmosphere, but just then, as Felix and I stood facing one another in silence, I felt a frantic desire to escape from the lift, which was carrying me to I knew not what, and to run down the stairs as fast as I could to the normal noise and congestion of the street outside.

We found Number Twelve on the second floor with a card in a slot beside it, giving Paul's name. Felix brought his piece of plastic out of his pocket, but before getting to work with it he observed, "You remember when Andrew arrived at the Appleyards' on Friday evening?"

"Yes," I said.

"Didn't you notice something rather odd at the time?"

"Several odd things. His being there at all, for one."

"Yes, but don't you remember how very casually he greeted Paul, just as if they'd met a day or two ago?"

"I suppose I do."

"He was only interested in Sonia and David."

"And his parents and Fran."

"But not in Paul, though they'd once been pretty good friends. That evening the two of them took hardly any notice of one another. I believe I've had a kind of feeling ever since then that there was something unnatural about it."

"That sounds to me like hindsight."

"Perhaps it is."

He turned to the door and did his best to slide the strip of plastic in beside the latch.

It did not work. Paul had a more sophisticated kind of lock than Sonia and David. After some futile fiddling with it Felix gave it up and produced a bunch of keys from his pocket. He tried one key after another without success and his face developed an irritated look of frustration.

Then suddenly there was a click, a key turned, and he opened the door.

Like David's flat, this consisted of a living-room, a bedroom, a bathroom, and a kitchen, but they were all on a smaller scale and had a muddled, unloved look about them. It seemed unlikely that Paul had ever enjoyed spending any time there. The basic furnishing was the limed oak of the twenties, which he had probably inherited from his parents or bought cheaply at some sale, and it was a long time since any polish had been used upon it and smears of dust lay on most of the surfaces. There were some files with papers bulging out of them on a table, and there were books lying on the floor, most of which seemed to be science fiction. There was a typewriter among the files.

Felix advanced into the living-room, went to the table, and with some caution began turning the papers in one of the files.

"If you'd tell me what we're looking for, perhaps I could help," I said.

"Evidence that Paul was married to Margaret Macinnes," he answered.

"You're sure he was?"

"Fairly sure."

"You think that letter in her handbag was typed on this typewriter?"

"It's possible. But the first thing is to see if we can find any paper that matches the paper that letter was written on. . . . Oh, here it is." He had moved a file and found under it a box of notepaper, and though we had seen only a photocopy of the letter, this at least seemed to be about the right size.

Felix slid a sheet of it into the typewriter and, as he had

done with David's, quickly typed a few lines from the letter we had seen.

"No! Don't try anything like that with me, Maggie. Perhaps I'll give you some help if I can, but not if you threaten me. . . ."

"Your memory!" I said.

He took the sheet of paper out of the typewriter.

"You see, she'd been trying to blackmail him, that's obvious," he said. "But he said she'd got nothing on him except that he'd kept quiet about what he had on her, and it certainly sounded in that letter Dawnay showed us as if what he had on her was bigamy. I believe she married Paul when they were both very young and someone who came in from the street and Andrew Appleyard were the witnesses. And Paul had taken the trouble to find out that the stranger was dead, and Andrew, away in America, seemed to have lost interest in what was happening here. But he came home at just the wrong time when Paul was getting ready to marry Andrew's sister Fran, and though Andrew might not have worried too much about a certain amount of bigamy among his old friends, it would probably have been different when it came to his own sister being caught up in it. So before Paul could propose to Fran, who I believe along with her other attractions happens to be a rich young woman, Andrew had to be got rid of. And unfortunately for him, he actually came here to spend the night with his old friend and perhaps even asked him questions about how his early marriage had worked out. So Paul knew he was going to Oldenham and had Thursday night to plan his murder and prepare his forged letter. But you see, if the engagement to Fran had never come off, if just possibly she'd turned him down, then Andrew's murder would have been sheer waste of effort. That's why I said Paul had had no motive for the murder until after it had happened."

"How did Margaret Macinnes know Paul wanted to marry Fran?"

"I suppose he told her. He must have been seeing something of her from time to time even after they separated. People sometimes do that, you know."

"I've always made it perfectly clear to you, Felix," I said, "that if you want to get married again, you can, but we'll have to have a divorce. I'm not playing around with bigamy."

"I know it, darling Virginia," he said, "and if ever I should think of taking that desperate step—"

He broke off as we heard the sound of a key turning in the door.

We both froze.

Then, after a moment, Felix whispered, "That porter knows we're here."

He went towards the door as it opened. I felt a shudder of panic as I thought of what Paul Camrose, a double murderer, might do when he found us there.

Detective Superintendent Dawnay stood in the doorway.

"So you got here before me," he said.

Sixteen

THE PORTER was on the landing behind the Superintendent. He pointed a finger at Felix and me and cried excitedly, "There they are! And I didn't let them in and they hadn't no search warrant! Ask them how they got in when Mr. Camrose wasn't here. Go on, ask them!"

But Superintendent Dawnay seemed hardly to be interested in how we had got into the flat. It was what had brought us there that he wanted explained. He had not come alone. Two large men who could only be plainclothes detectives followed him in. Whether they had come with him from Allingford or were members of the Metropolitan police I never found out, but after a few words from him they began a quiet search of the flat. Meanwhile he looked at Felix and said, "What put you on to him?"

"That letter you showed us that made it fairly certain that either Camrose or Eldred was involved in bigamy," Felix answered.

"And what made you pick on Camrose?" the Superintendent asked.

Felix chose not to mention our fruitless visit to David's flat. He preferred to be given the credit for having chosen the right one straight away. But perhaps it was true that he had known what he was doing and had wanted to try David's flat only in order to eliminate him.

"I thought the relationship between Eldred and Miss Capel being as well known as it is, there'd have been no need for him to risk a quite unnecessary marriage just for the hell of it, so to speak," he said. "If in fact he'd ever been married to Margaret McNair, I was inclined to think, Sonia Capel would have been told all about it long ago. In fact, I did wonder if it could have been the reason why the two of them hadn't got married. But then why the marriage now? So Camrose seemed the likelier option. And perhaps this will be of use to you."

Felix held out the few lines of typing that he had executed on the typewriter here a few minutes before.

The Superintendent took it, glanced at it, nodded, and put it into his wallet, but then went to the typewriter himself, slid a sheet of the notepaper on the table into it, and as Felix and I looked over his shoulder to see what he would write, typed the words, "There were three jovial huntsmen and a-hunting they did go, and they hunted and they hollered and they blew their horns also, look 'ee there!"

"Is that how you think of yourself?" I asked. "A jovial huntsman?"

"No, it was just the first thing that came into my head," he answered as he added the sheet to what was already in his wallet, "though the three of us being here together perhaps . . . Nothing very jovial about my work most of the time, but I needed something to check the typing, naturally, and didn't want to confuse it with your husband's work or the original. Now what about telling me some more about why you're here."

I left it to Felix to do that. What he told the Superintendent was more or less what he had told me just before the police had arrived concerning his belief that it was Paul who had killed Andrew Appleyard and his reason for doing so. As he spoke I began to think of Fran, but I found that that was something which almost would not bear thinking about. She was in love, was so radiantly happy, was so full of hope and confidence. My mind wandered and it was only as Felix ended his statement that it came back to the subject of the moment.

Felix had ended abruptly with the question, "And now may I ask what brought you here, Superintendent?"

"Evidence," the detective answered.

"Ah," Felix said, "I see. And you don't think I'd much of that."

"I think what you've got, Mr. Freer, is something of great value, a very active imagination," Superintendent Dawnay replied. "It often leads the way to the right conclusion, but unsupported, it isn't much use in a court of law."

"Oddly enough, I've never been in a court of law in my life," Felix said. And in a way, I thought, it really was rather odd. He had never been into one out of mere curiosity as a member of the public, or as a witness, or as a defendant, though the last was something that I had feared for years. "But this evidence you've got, are you going to tell us anything about it?"

"No reason I shouldn't, but it's just odds and ends at present," the Superintendent said, "though they seem to add up to something. First, there were some pieces of broken glass that we found on the bank of the river Olden. It looked as if someone had intended to throw the whole glass into the river, but his aim was bad and it bounced on a stone at the water's edge and shattered. Some of it went into the stream, but some of it stayed scattered around the stone and one or two of the pieces are large enough to show finger-prints and they happen to be Mr. Camrose's. Also, pieced together, it's evident that the glass matches some others that are kept in the guest bungalow at Oldenham House. A glass was missing from there, we'd been told by the servant Martha, and this seemed to be it. Camrose, we think, had a drink with Appleyard, whose brandy was well laced with the drug Camrose had picked up at Arne Webster, knew that his prints would be on the glass he'd drunk from, and sooner than risk waking you by washing it there in the bungalow, took it away with him and did his best to dispose of it."

Felix nodded thoughtfully. "I've always thought that glass would turn out to be important, ever since Martha told me about it. And what other odds and ends have you?"

"A telephone call a woman made to The Barley Mow on Saturday evening, not giving her name but leaving a message for Camrose, asking him to telephone a number in Allingford. The number happened to be that of a small hotel called The Kingsway, where the McNair woman had checked in earlier in the day, after failing to get a room at The Barley Mow. A call for her came through about eleven o'clock and she immediately went out and never returned. We presume she arranged during that call where she was to pick up Camrose in her Mini so that she could tell him what the price would be for her silence, and he was picked up by her and they drove around for a while till he found what he thought was a suitable place to kill her, did the job, and from there walked back to The Barley Mow. Our only evidence that it was Camrose who made the call to The Kingsway is that he was seen by a witness making a call from the telephone kiosk in the village about eleven o'clock, which may not be absolutely conclusive, as he had his key to The Barley Mow and his comings and goings weren't observed. We haven't found any blood-stained clothing yet, but something may turn up. However, we've the evidence of the Appleyards' chauffeur."

"Bob?" Felix said. "Ah yes, I think I know what you mean. When the woman in pink first turned up at Oldenham House, she spoke to Bob, didn't she, and asked him if it was true that Eldred and Camrose were staying at the house? He told her they weren't, but were staying at the pub, and I think we all assumed it was Eldred she was interested in, but in fact she'd asked for Camrose too. That's a bit slender, isn't it?"

"Yes, but it all adds up. What we still need is evidence of the marriage between Camrose and McNair, but it shouldn't be hard to find now we know what we're looking for."

He did not tell us then that he already had what, if it was not proof that Paul had married Margaret McNair, at least made it look more than probable. Before coming to Paul's flat, he and his followers had already been to hers in Islington, and though she had not kept the certificate of her first marriage, she had apparently not been able to make herself destroy a photograph in which he and she were standing together, smiling blandly at the photographer, and though she was not in a wedding dress, she was holding a bouquet of flowers and had a distinctly bridal air. I never saw the photograph, but I heard that it was only a snapshot, not a professional job, and I could not help wondering if it had been Andrew Appleyard who had held the camera. Actually it did not take the police long to trace the registration of the marriage, but even before they had done that Paul had been taken in for questioning. He had been taken to the police station in Allingford while Felix and I were in London, though he was not charged until the next day.

We did not have dinner at The Rose and Crown when we arrived home in the evening. It would have been a total waste of money. We should have sat facing one another, almost entirely silent, for there would have been very little that we should have felt able to talk about while we had the eyes of waiters and other diners upon us. We did not have to discuss with one another what we should do, Felix simply drove to Ellsworthy Street and we went into the house and he poured out drinks for us both, then asked if I could face another omelette.

I was grateful for the suggestion and said that it struck me as the best thing that we could have, then settled down with the whisky that I was drinking while he swallowed his sherry quickly, then disappeared to the kitchen. Cooking had always had a therapeutic effect on him. It did not surprise me when presently he returned to the sitting-room, pushing my tea-trolley with a beautifully made Spanish omelette on it, as well as a salad and coffee. But although we were by ourselves, we seemed to have almost nothing to say to one another. I could not stop thinking about Fran, but I did not find that I could talk about her.

In the end, when I had stacked our plates in the dishwasher, I suddenly said, "You needn't come, Felix, but I'm going out to Oldenham."

"Oh, I'll come," he said. "That's what I've been thinking about myself."

"Do you think they know everything by now?" I asked.

"If they don't, there's no need for us to tell them anything," he said.

"You don't think I should tell even Christine what's been happening?"

"Oh no, that's strictly a job for the police."

"But if Paul's there, with Fran . . ."

"Treat him as you'd treat any normal member of the

human race. I suppose he isn't normal, but one isn't advised to take too much notice of that nowadays. It's said to help the insane if one can absorb them into the community."

"Poor old community! And I'm not sure if I want to help Paul."

"I'm not too enthusiastic about it myself, but I'd hate to get involved in some fearful scene with him because of that. We can say we just came to see how they all were, then come away quietly. They may actually prefer it if we don't stick around."

I thought that after all that was quite likely and even if Paul was still there with them he was not going to do any more harm to anyone. Going out to the street, we got into Felix's car once more and he drove us out to Oldenham. The long twilight of the summer evening had almost faded into darkness and stars were beginning to shine in the deep blue of the sky. Before we were half way to Oldenham I had begun to wish that we had not come, for what could we do for the people there who had had time now to begin to feel their real grief at Andrew's death, murdered while he had been plotting murder, as apart from reacting to the shock of it. But I did not say anything about this and presently we reached the Appleyards' house.

It was Christine who opened the door to us when I rang the doorbell. She stared at us for a moment as if she did not know who we were, but she had opened the door so quickly after we arrived that I thought that she must have been waiting near it, expecting someone. Then I realised that this had probably been the police, which might mean that they had already taken Paul away with them, and I felt sure of this when, after the first moment of hesitation, she clutched me by both arms and hauled me indoors. Felix followed me in.

"Oh, Virginia, a terrible thing has happened," she said in a shaking voice. "I can't take it in. Martha has given notice!"

After that she burst into tears and hid her face against me.

This was worse than I had expected. I had always known that Christine was a very highly strung woman, but I had never before seen her in such a state of hysteria. I put my arms round her, wondering what on earth I was to do. What I said was drearily banal.

"Well, that isn't the end of the world, is it? You'll find someone else."

"It's the last straw," she sobbed. "To do it to us now! I always thought she was quite fond of us, but she came to me today and said she'd been offered a job at half again as much as we've been paying her by a single gentleman in the West End and that she'd always had a fancy to work in London. But I don't think it's really because of that that she's going. After all, if she thought we were underpaying her, she'd only to tell us so and she'd always seemed quite happy here in the country. I think it's because of the murders and the police coming and going and Paul being arrested all of a sudden. Did you know that?" She suddenly raised her head and looked at me. "Did you know they've arrested Paul?"

"Actually arrested him?" I said. "Not just taken him in for questioning?"

"It's the same thing, isn't it?" she said. "And we know he's guilty because of the way he behaved when they came for him. He started to shout and rage and he caught hold of Fran and held her in front of him and yelled that he'd break her neck and throw her into the pool if anyone touched him. It was she who talked him out of it. She didn't try to struggle with him but said quite gently that she wished he would throw her into the pool because what she wanted most was to drown, and that seemed to calm him and he went away with the police quite quietly."

Christine had grown calmer herself by now, had withdrawn from my embrace and begun to mop her eyes.

"I'm so sorry," she said. "It's absurd of me to be so upset about Martha at a time like this, isn't it? It's just finding that everyone—yes, everyone—is different from what I've always thought. But as you say, we'll find someone else sooner or later, but we'll never have the same sort of feelings about her, and I can't help wondering if Mrs. Grantly won't find the work too hard for her till we do find someone and perhaps she'll leave too. How lucky you are, Virginia, having such a comfortable little house which you can cope with quite easily yourself. You don't know how I envy you."

This was Christine who only earlier on the same day had told me how lucky she herself was because she had had George with her over the years, which at the time had given me a sharp pang of envy, though I hoped that I had not shown it.

"Now come in, both of you," she said, and as Felix closed the front door, which had remained open behind us, led the way into the drawing-room.

George and Fran were there and the chessboard and chessmen were set out on their table, as if someone had thought that a game of chess might be a good idea, but then had not had the heart to play. The french window was open and Sonia and David were sitting on the terrace beside the pool, which once more was an oblong of darkness, touched with silver.

Fran was sitting on the sofa, her elbows on her knees,

her chin cupped in her hands. Her fresh young face had the grey pallor of someone very old and tired. Her eyes were wide open and staring as if they were focussed on something a long way away. She did not look towards us as we entered or show that she was aware of there being anyone else in the room with her.

George was standing in front of the empty fireplace with his bulging eyes wide open too, but full of a puzzled desperation as he gazed down helplessly at his daughter. The moment that Felix and I came into the room he began speaking to us, almost as if we had been there in the room with him for some time.

"She won't talk, you know, she won't listen to anything one says to her. I've told her we don't really know anything yet, they may be all wrong, they may not convict. She doesn't answer, she doesn't seem to have heard one. It's shock, of course, and I can't help wondering if we ought to call Dr. Burrows to come and give her something. Can you say anything to her, Virginia? My father-in-law tried but he's given up and he's gone upstairs to lie down. She just looked through him. Please see if you can at least get her to listen to you."

It seemed to me that there was nothing to be done until the worst of the shock had worn off and the girl allowed herself to suffer what in the end she would have to face. But it was difficult to say anything of the sort with her there before us and I could not think of anything else to say.

Lamely, I said what I could. "We only came to ask if there's anything we can do to help and to say how sorry we are that things have turned out as they have."

"I know, I know," Christine said in the high voice that she tended to use when she was agitated, and going to George she put her arms round him, clinging to him, either to give him support or to be supported herself, it was difficult to tell which. Perhaps in spite of everything they were to some extent lucky people, because they were so sure of one another. "Of course she'll get over it, she's so young, just give her a little time. After all, they hardly knew one another. Fran, darling . . ." But then she paused, as if she had realised that it was no use trying to talk to that immobile figure on the sofa, that its ears were probably as deaf as its eyes were blind.

Whether being so young would in fact help Fran at all, or do its opposite, I did not know. Fran herself, in one of her psychological moods, would probably have claimed that it was the wounds inflicted on the young that leave scars for a lifetime.

At that moment there was the sound of running footsteps in the hall behind us and Ilse came bounding into the room. She did not hesitate for an instant but flung herself down on the sofa beside Fran, threw her arms round her, and pulled her towards her.

"Fran, you come with me," she said, "you come away with me to Zurich. You come away from everything here. I telephone my brother Kurt and he will meet us at the airport. You stay with us as long as you like. We go tomorrow, or if you cannot go tomorrow, the first day they let you go. You need not tell anyone there what has happened to you. Yes, you come with me to Zurich. You were happy there."

Suddenly Fran's frightening rigidity dissolved. Giving a strange eerie wail, she buried her face on the other girl's shoulder as her whole body began to shake with frantic sobs.

"Thank God for that," George muttered. "Thank you, Ilse."

"You let her come with me to Zurich?" Ilse asked, gently stroking Fran's hair.

"To the moon, if that'll help her," he answered.

"Good, good. She likes Kurt. Kurt will help her."

"I think this is where we slip softly away," Felix murmured in my ear, and without saying good-bye to anyone, the two of us quietly withdrew from the room.

When we were outside in the drive where we had left Felix's car, I went towards it, but instead of going with me, Felix said, "Just a moment. I want a word with Bob."

"Bob? Why Bob?" I asked.

"An idea I had, something that might help a little," Felix answered, and set off rapidly in the direction of the garages.

I followed him, wondering what he could have to say to Bob at a time like this. I was also wondering whether Felix would be staying the night with me, or would be setting off shortly for Little Carbery Street. That was what I was really expecting and rather hoping that he would do. I knew that I would miss him for a little while after he had gone, as I always sadly do after one of his brief visits, but I knew also that if he stayed we might soon find ourselves perilously close to trying to mend our broken relationship, the end of which would be disaster. We had been through that sort of thing too often for me to have any hope that I could really endure more than a little of him at a time.

We found Bob in his room above the garages. He was in jeans and nothing else and looked brown and healthy and strong, though his face was grave. He invited us into the room, but Felix stayed at the top of the stairs that led up to it and I stayed a few steps below him, curious to hear why he had come.

"Bob, d'you feel like helping those people in there?" he asked, nodding towards the house.

"Anything I can do," Bob replied readily.

"You know they're in pretty terrible trouble," Felix said.

"That's right," Bob agreed. "Terrible. Like I said, anything I can do."

"Well, you know Martha's leaving, don't you?" Felix went on. "And Mrs. Appleyard's very upset about it. I thought if you'd go and offer to push the vacuum cleaner around the house to help out for a time, it might sort of cheer her up a little. Show good will and so on, if you care about them."

"Ah, I get it," Bob said. "Sure, I can do that."

"Thank you."

"My pleasure," Bob said. "No problem."

As Felix and I drove back to Allingford I reflected that in its small way it was reassuring to think there was at least one person in that household too solidly sane to be overpowered by its problems.

E. X. FERRARS, who lives in England, is the author of over sixty works of mystery and suspense, including *Smoke Without Fire* and *Woman Slaughter*. She has received a special award from the British Crime Writers Association for continuing excellence in the mystery field.